PENGUIN BOOKS
SERENDIPITY

Ashok Ferrey is the author of five books, four of them nominated for the Gratiaen Prize and the fifth for the State Literary Award. By day he is a personal trainer.

GW00648159

ALSO BY ASHOK FERREY

Serendipity

ASHOK FERREY

PENGUIN BOOKS

An imprint of Penguin Random House

PENGUIN BOOKS

USA | Canada | UK | Ireland | Australia
New Zealand | India | South Africa | China

Penguin Books is part of the Penguin Random House group of companies
whose addresses can be found at global.penguinrandomhouse.com

Published by Penguin Random House India Pvt. Ltd
7th Floor, Infinity Tower C, DLF Cyber City,
Gurgaon 122 002, Haryana, India

Penguin
Random House
India

First published in Vintage by Random House India 2009
Published in Penguin Books by Penguin Random House India 2017

10 9 8 7 6 5 4 3 2

This is a work of fiction. Names, characters, places and incidents are
either the product of the author's imagination or are used fictitiously, and
any resemblance to any actual person, living or dead, events or locales
is entirely coincidental.

ISBN 9780143440161

For sale in the Indian Subcontinent only

Typeset in Linden Hill Regular by SÜRYA, New Delhi
Printed at Repro Knowledgecast Limited, India

www.penguin.co.in

For Tilly,
with love and respect

Serendipity: serendipity/n. the occurrence and development of events by chance in a happy or beneficial way.

—Origin 1754: Coined by Horace Walpole, suggested by *The Three Princes of Serendip*, the title of a fairy tale in which the heroes were always making fortunate discoveries.

The Concise Oxford Dictionary

AUTHOR'S NOTE

History is of necessity the interpretation of an assorted chocolate box of facts, foil-wrapped and brightly coloured, the same assortment giving rise to as many interpretations as there are historians. The events in this book are not real, nor do they take place in real time: so they are not a part of anybody's history and should not be seen as such. They are merely the kaleidoscopic fragments of an author's fervid imagination, falling this way and that, now forming a pattern, now not; sometimes giving rise to a pretty picture we might want to call serendipity. Sometimes not.

A. F.

1

'Boom!'

Mrs Herath was in the garden of her Deal Place home in Colombo, harvesting bandakka when the bomb went off. She looked around for debris. Last time, a fine sheen of steel ball-bearings had shimmered all over the front lawn like stars in the southern sky. It had taken weeks to get them out: they were impervious to rake and broom and they ruined the blades of Mr Herath's hand-held lawn-mower.

This time she could see nothing. No debris.

Inside the house her husband had woken up from his nap. 'What was that, dear?'

'Nothing, dear. Just a bomb.'

It was only then she discovered, nestling among the tender green fingers of okra, a freshly severed thumb. It was pinky-brown, the colour of old rose.

'How very careless of me,' she said. 'I seem to have harvested a thumb.'

'Silly old bat,' muttered her husband. He never believed any of her improbable stories.

'What was that, dear?'

'Nothing, dear. I just said, these days you seem to be all thumbs.'

It had been different when they were in London . . . now home was Deal Place, Colombo. But it was different here, too. The Sri Lanka they had returned to had churned and turned into a new dish they hardly recognized. At least the weather was the same. Those of their compatriots who'd left for a better life had certainly not left for better climes.

There was almost no difference between the dreary London winter cold outside and the dim green fluorescence of the shop's interior. But you forgave anything in a shop that stayed open all hours. Well, almost anything. Piyumi reached into the rusty freezer cabinet to get the last carton of guava juice. It was bloated and heavy and quite probably way past its sell-by date. She was tempted to examine the small writing on the carton and put it back, but she felt Mr Skanda's gentle but implacable eyes boring into her back. Returning it would have been tantamount to an insult.

'We are from the same country,' he had stated quite simply, when she first walked into the shop. How he knew was anyone's guess because she hadn't even told him her name. But there was a heavy weight of obligation behind the statement, unspoken, and as yet unfulfilled. They were both immigrants: they belonged to the same club.

She was too polite to mention that back home they were most definitely not of the same club: there was a vast ocean of difference between a high-caste Jaffna Tamil girl from a grand Hindu family and a poor Catholic of the coastal fisherman caste. How she knew all this in that same silent instant was anyone's guess too. But she did. That was the way it was in Sri Lanka.

'If you don't want that, can I have it?'

A young man had seen her hesitating over the bloated carton. He was pale and freckled, with coarse sandy hair. His wrists, she noticed, were painfully thin. She also vaguely noted that he couldn't be English. This was another thing she knew intuitively.

'No,' she said hurriedly, finally coming to a decision. 'I do.'

She paid Mr Skanda, nodded at the stranger and walked out. Her patent leather shoes pinched, her black tights were crooked. This was always the moment of the day when she longed to throw herself wearily into a waiting tuk-tuk and say, 'Drive me home, Margolis (or Sirisena, or Justin).' Instead, she walked, creak, creak, up High Street, took a turn into Venn Street, creak, creak, and down the slope into Triangle Place. The red brick of the council flats looked strangely cheering after the gloom of High Street. Through the glass doors of the front entrance (only good to keep honest people out) and up the concrete stairway to her own door, painted green in a vain effort to disguise the cracking and gouging around the lock. It had been broken so often by yobs in the neighbourhood, it wasn't worth replacing.

It was so unfair, she thought. She was almost always the

one called upon in her legal firm to defend these men when their cases came up. Only this morning, there had been two blokes accused of stealing a TV from an old woman who lived in the same block as they did. They had run off with it in broad daylight, in full view of everyone. She had got them off on a technicality—a brilliant piece of defence. But throughout the proceedings, she had been aware, even if the jury wasn't, of their previous convictions. All eleven of them.

Tariq was sprawled on the sofa with his feet up on the coffee table, the remains of a pile of barbecued spare ribs in front of him arranged on a plate like the timbers of a cathedral roof.

'I got hungry, love.' He caught her as she went past, burying his unshaven face into her skirt. She could feel the prickles of his beard through the wool.

'So how's my little black barrister then? All ready for a debriefing?'

Pushing past him she went into the open kitchen. 'Your mother called,' he said. 'Wants us to come over for Sunday lunch. I said you're free.'

'And you're not?'

He burped. 'You know how I get busy on Sundays.' She poured a quarter cup of basmati into the rice cooker. It hadn't always been like this. She thought about the little green enamelled glass bracelet he had brought back from Pakistan in the early days. *I'll always love you. You're the only one for me.*

Love is a rock, she thought, an island lying far out in a vast ocean of clichés. Now you see it, now you don't. Just when you think you've rowed up to it, you find you're actually nowhere near. There are so many more clichés to go.

Piyumi began chopping onions and garlic. A little yellow rice, a little chicken curry—for one.

Marek's mother was lying in the great big bed in the front room on the first floor overlooking the street. The curtains, heavy pink and brocade, were drawn and the air was sweet with the smell of rosewater and stale sweat. It was the lair of a large animal already hunkered down for its winter hibernation. He could hardly breathe.

'Marek,' she called. 'Marek. Where's my guava juice then?'

He shook his head. 'There wasn't any. Some girl took the last carton.'

He could have easily got some at the Sainsbury's across the road. But he liked to inflict these little cruelties on her from time to time, refined and sensuous, like so many sushi on a plate. It was what kept him going through all this ugliness.

'Never mind, dear. You can get me some tomorrow.' She took his hand. He couldn't stand it when she forgave him. Hate me! he wanted to shout. Hate me!

Her boiled blue eyes glittered for a moment with suspicion. 'You'll never leave me, will you dear?'

'No, Ma.' He shook his head knowing how she took comfort in his little lies.

Mr Ridoynauth downstairs began practising his drums.

'Tell him to stop, dear. Tell him I have a bit of a headache.'

As he opened their door to go downstairs, two young guys

came bounding down from the flat above, lithe and sleek as gazelles. They looked at him briefly with liquid eyes and continued down. There was an awful lot of coming and going upstairs today, he thought. You never knew how many people lived up there, they were so quiet most of the time.

There had been a time when the entire house belonged to Marek's father. A few months before he died he had called Marek into his room, the same big front room his mother was now in.

'I worry about her,' he whispered. 'I don't know who'll look after her when I'm gone.'

'I will,' Marek replied boldly. 'I will.'

It was the only conversation they had ever had man to man.

Months later he was dead and the first thing she did was to sell the floor above. Then the floor below.

'Flats in Tremadoc Road are really valuable,' she told him.

'So why are you selling, then?' He was only sixteen, he didn't have much of a say in the matter.

Her eyes lit up. 'For you, dear, who else? I'm putting all the money into the bank so you'll never want for any. You're safe now, dear, you can relax.'

Six months later the flat below had been resold by the new buyer for nearly double the amount;the one above went a month later for twice what she had got. Marek watched all these new occupants come and go. He smiled and smiled through his pain.

2

Piyumi's mother lived in an Art Deco block of flats in Knightsbridge—another country as far as Piyumi was concerned. A Sinhalese, Mrs Segarajasingham had married her Tamil husband in those heady post-independence days when upper classes of the two communities had actually much more in common with each other than with less fortunate members of their own communities. The Sinhala Only policy of the fifties followed by successive race riots had, however, driven a wedge deep between the two. She had moved to London in the eighties, having conveniently disposed of her husband in a week of particularly vicious rioting that took place in Colombo: at least that is how she described it to her posh London friends. In fact, he had died a few months later, peacefully in his sleep of old age. (He had been much older.) But she had found him to be something of a disappointment; it seemed to her only fair that in death he should end up where he now was: as an after-dinner joke in the worst possible taste.

The riots of the eighties began when separatist Tamil Tigers ambushed and massacred a convoy of thirteen Sinhala soldiers, and a Sinhala president steadfastly turned a blind eye to the ensuing riots. The Segarajasinghams hid under the bed of their frightfully common neighbours, the loudly braying Rodrigos, and returned to their own home a week later, unharmed.

Mrs Segar (she shortened her surname thereafter) never forgave Sri Lanka, or indeed Sri Lankans, for this outrage perpetrated on her person. In those days, the Sri Lankan rupee was convertible on the black market into hard currency, and she converted big time. The houses, the estates, all were exchanged in one glorious sweep for two dreary Knightsbridge flats.

It was an area beyond reproach. More importantly for Mrs Segar, it was an area beyond immigration. London to her was the centre of the world, the Imperial Capital. It didn't seem fair to her then that it should be peopled by those of a skin colour darker than her own. ('He may be from Colombo 7, dear, but he's black.') Profoundly beautiful, with a skin the colour of pale alabaster, she was the sort of Sri Lankan who would swiftly cross the road when she saw a fellow countryman approaching. Knightsbridge was thankfully free of such hazards. But, alas, things were changing. There were Arabs in the flats now (swarthy people) and they employed Sri Lankan nannies. Can you believe it, dear, Sri Lankan nannies? Mrs Segar carried on regardless, in her sensible court shoes, her shapeless tweeds, the heirloom emeralds re-cut and re-set to look like costume junk.

This then was the hand Piyumi had been dealt at birth, till one day she threw all her cards up in the air and walked out—

to a flat of her own south of the river, in another country called Brixton.

It was raining in Knightsbridge.

'I knew you'd be sick of curry, curry, curry,' said Mrs Segar. 'So I've baked us a shepherd's pie.' The mashed potato was grey, the meat was grey. There was no salt or anything remotely resembling seasoning. (It was a Knightsbridge recipe.) Looking closely, Piyumi realized that actually there was no meat either.

'Meat is bad for my heart,' explained Mrs Segar. 'So I've used soya products.' Piyumi failed to see how even a soya product could help a woman who had been heartless most of her life.

'I think it tastes just the same, don't you?' There was no answer so Mrs Segar continued, 'Aunty Chelvam has died.'

Piyumi wanted to say, My love has died, but it was no time for levity. She watched spurts of rain fizz and flare against the window like match flames.

'She's left us the kitchen quarters. Someone's got to go back and represent us.'

'I'll go,' said Piyumi—a little too quickly—and instantly regretted it. It was never wise to express too much interest if you really wanted something. Far better to say no, and gradually work your way round to a yes. For all her Englishness, Mrs Segar was a thoroughly Sri Lankan strategist.

'You? What use would you be? Don't you have a job?' Piyumi thought of her chambers, the florid men with thinning hair who wasted no opportunity telling her how lucky she was to get the job, a woman in a man's world and a coloured one at that. Work was sparse. An occasional pro bono bone was thrown in her direction when everyone else at table had finished with it. The men were sympathetic to her plight, but they didn't invite her to go drinking with them after hours. She could do with a few weeks' holiday.

'Why would you want to go anyway?' asked her mother. 'It's a banana republic. The trains don't run on time.'

'Because it's home.'

'Home? Home?' asked Mrs Segar incredulously. 'This is home!'

'For you maybe. For me it'll always be there.'

It was a source of regret to Mrs Segar that she had reared such a traditional, backward-looking Asian child.

It was her fault, of course, entirely her fault. She was far too loyal to say so, but in many ways she would have preferred an English daughter who left home at sixteen and came back once a year at Christmas, tattooed and pregnant.

'How can you call that home? You're half-Tamil!' There it was. Sooner or later, in any conversation, someone said it. The subject lay between them like a beached whale, dead and putrefying. Nothing about it improved in the retelling.

'I never regretted leaving Sri Lanka,' said Piyumi's mother. 'I could never live like a second-class citizen in my own country.'

'Far better,' said Piyumi wearily, 'to live like a second-class citizen in someone else's.'

It was still raining when she left Knightsbridge. Mr Skanda was busy evicting rust spots from his ancient freezer unit. There was no guava juice today, the deliveries hadn't come.

'We have a small group of Sri Lankans,' Mr Skanda said. 'We involve ourselves in charity work back home.' He paused. 'We meet once a week, Wednesday evenings at seven. Number 8, Tremadoc Road.'

It wasn't a request, she realized. More in the way of an order. She wanted to say, I have better things to do on a Wednesday evening. Instead she bought a quarter-pound of chillies and fled.

3

Number 8 had always been the best kept house on Tremadoc Road, Marek's father being that rarest of creatures, the house-proud builder. Even more unusual was his love of old things: the cornices, the fireplaces, the quartered doors, all remained intact in a time which favoured smoothness and blandness in all things architectural.

His mother was a different fish altogether. It was no surprise, therefore, that the first things to go when his father died were the fireplaces.

'I couldn't stand them draughty old things,' she said. 'I got fifty quid apiece.' She caught his look. 'Don't you worry, my little pet. It all goes into a savings account for you.' She squeezed his cheek.

It was the glorious blue-rinsed Thatcher Eighties then, and building sites were springing up like acne all over the face of that area of south London that was really neither Brixton nor Clapham. Marek got a holiday job with Ernie, one of the builders down the road. He knew nothing about building. But then Ernie didn't either. That was the way it was in the Thatcher Years. The less you knew the more money you made.

Less is more, they kept telling you.

They moved from site to site, up and down the nearby streets, a sort of travelling gypsy encampment. He found great peace of mind in labouring. Your mind wandered far and free, while your body submitted itself to the tyranny of the pick-axe and shovel and the 50-kilo cement bag.('Come on, you greasy Pole!' Ernie would shout from the roof as he climbed up the scaffolding with packs of artificial slates on his shoulder.) At the end of the day, he'd sit swinging his legs over the edge of the scaffold, drinking milk from a carton while the roofs around him turned pink in the sunset, his hands glowing with the stigmata of their blisters and their pain.

All through his history degree he worked on sites whenever he could. Even now when he was looking for a proper job, in the real world, he couldn't decide where he wanted to be. History for him was solely the study of people's motives: the actions behind their words. So much could be explained, not by the facts and figures historians were fond of touting, but by the far simpler truths of greed or lust or treachery. And then, of course, there was serendipity: those happy accidents of chance that diverted the crackling currents of destiny at the flick of a switch.

Ernie was the only one left on site when he got there.

'Cup of tea?'

'Don't mind if I do.'

They sat on a scaffold board in companionable silence. 'Jobs?'

'Three rejections so far, one no-show,' he replied moodily.

'Your employer didn't bother to show up?' Ernie asked incredulously.

'I didn't! I got to the place, walked round a bit, decided I couldn't face it.'

Ernie knew better than to ask why. There was more silence.

'How's your mother?'

Everyone up and down these roads knew his mother. She was the stuff of legend and history. She never left the house. On summer evenings she raised the sashes of her room high and held court at her window, talking down to whoever cared to listen. It was like an audience with the Pope. The Polish Pope of Clapham. Marek looked at his watch. 'I'd best be getting back to her.'

He couldn't decide where home was. Deep in the de Tocqueville of his history books, or the Victorian drains of the building site. He knew where it wasn't: at Number 8, Tremadoc Road.

4

'How long will you be gone? Two weeks? Two months?'
Piyumi shrugged.

'And what am I supposed to do while you're gone?' he asked.

'I don't know. You figure it out.' There's some sort of
telepathy between people who live together, she thought. He
was ready with his quarrel when I walked in.

Wednesdays were always tough on her. The weekly
chambers' meeting, when they gave their progress report to
the senior partners in front of everyone else: the suppressed
sniggers, the patronizing looks (look everyone, hasn't our girl
done well?). Her offerings were always painfully meagre.

'Who's going to pay the bills?'

'You are,' she said with a grim smile. 'You'll get off your
backside and go get a job, any job. There are tons of building
sites around.'

'But my hands . . .' he said. Tariq was a writer. His hands
were precious. He was precious.

'Fuck your hands,' she wanted to say but somehow that
sounded too intimate.

'Fucking bitch,' he growled, 'what's for dinner?' You could always tell the quarrel was coming to an end when he got abusive. This time she didn't want it to end.

'You tell me,' she said. 'Because you're cooking.' She slammed the door on her way out.

Oh, Tariq! Tariq! she thought, how did it ever come to this?

There were five of them sitting there, talking in Tamil when she arrived, five men. They looked up guiltily, like children caught by their mother imparting secrets to the servants.

'It's okay,' she said, 'I can hardly speak Tamil.'

There were four plastic chairs around a formica table. The bare floorboards were covered by linoleum. At one corner, to complete the arrangement, was a fluorescent orange armchair adding a note of slightly hysterical levity to the proceedings. On it sat Mr Skanda.

'Didn't your mother teach you?' he asked gently.

'We only ever spoke Sinhala and Tamil to the servants,' she said, not willing to expound her mother's view on natives. 'Everything else was in English.' She smiled apologetically, wondering as she did why she felt the need to justify herself.

They were drinking coffee out of pottery mugs, the five of them. Nobody offered her any and nobody offered her a chair. She sat on the floor.

'You're going to Colombo,' Mr Skanda said.

'Am I? Goodness, news travels fast!' she replied lightly.

Mr Skanda did not smile. 'You move in the sort of circles,' said Mr Skanda choosing his words carefully, 'the sort of circles we don't normally have access to . . .' Piyumi looked at the others in the group. They were all in their twenties or thirties. They looked back at her with unblinking eyes and it dawned on her they didn't speak a word of English.

'When you go back,' said Mr Skanda, 'we would like you to help us with our charity work.'

'Charity work? Charity work?' Her laughter rang out hollow in that bare room. Nobody laughed with her. 'You want me to be some sort of spy?'

Mr Skanda looked pained. 'No, no, nothing as dramatic as that,' he said sadly. 'We would just like you to keep us updated on certain things.' He looked at the others as if for support, but they stared back motionless. 'And if you need transport while you're out there, we can arrange it.'

'That's my carrot, is it?'

He ignored her levity. 'Just keep in touch, that's all.'

Marek saw them as they came downstairs. At first he couldn't place Mr Skanda in his long cashmere coat, looking like some sort of king-emperor in exile. Then he saw the girl.

'Back for more guava juice, then?'

She looked up and smiled. 'You live here?'

He was standing outside his own doorway. He wanted to ask her in. He thought of his mother indoors. (Marek, Marek, who's that with you? Bring them in, will you, I want to have a look.)

'My mother's not well,' he said regretfully.

Mr Skanda moved past them. He began to descend the staircase, a strange king and his courtiers.

'I'm so used to seeing you in your shop,' Marek called out after him. 'I didn't recognize you in these strange surroundings.'

Mr Skanda looked back at him. 'These are not strange surroundings,' he said simply. 'That flat belongs to me.' After he had gone, Marek said to her: 'Do you want to go out somewhere, maybe get a drink or something?' He had never been so bold with a girl in his life. The fact that she was not English made her less intimidating somehow.

She hesitated, then looked at her watch. 'My boyfriend's cooking dinner.'

'Boyfriend?' He was crushed.

'Maybe another time? If you give me your number . . .' He scribbled it down for her, and she smiled again.

'. . . I'll give you a call.'

He waited till she had gone, then opened his front door. Almost immediately the voice began. 'Marek,' it said, 'Marek.' An automatic response, like an ingenious burglar alarm, a sort of electronic parrot. 'I've cooked you a nice bit of gammon. It's there in the oven.'

He didn't bother to answer. He walked down the corridor to the back-addition kitchen. The piece of gammon lay surrounded by boiled potatoes and boiled frozen peas. She hadn't drained them properly and there was half an inch of water in the plate. He knew she was listening. As quietly as he could he opened the bin and scraped it all off the plate, taking care to cover it well with the other rubbish. She had been known to root about in there next day to check if he had really eaten what she had cooked.

He went quietly to his own room and began to undress. The phone rang. It was her. He could feel his breath quickening and his heart begin to pound.

'Can you come quickly? Please! Something's happened.' She gave him the address in Triangle Place. 'Do you know where that is?'

Putting the phone down, he ran.

She buzzed him in and he took the steps two at a time. The green door was ajar. He found her sitting on the sofa, about the only thing that was upright, weeping quietly.

'I'm sorry,' she said between sobs, 'you were the only one I could think to call.'

Her law books were all over the floor, the TV toppled over. He put his arms around her and hugged her, rocking her back and forth gently. There was a deep red stain on the carpet. She saw him looking at it. 'Oh, it's not blood,' she said. 'He's emptied the bottle of ketchup.'

'Have you called the police?'

She shook her head. 'What's the point? I know where he's gone. Back to his family. He didn't take anything. Only some money I had in the bedroom.'

'Only money,' he said wryly. They began putting stuff back, the books, the TV. In the bedroom her clothes were all pulled out of racks, the drawers emptied out on the floor.

He began folding things and putting them back, her jewellery, her underwear. I hardly know her, he thought, yet I already know more about her than most of her friends. The strange familiarity of it all made him sad. He was starting out at the wrong end of the story.

She turned on the bathroom light and screamed.

On the mirror in pink lipstick was written, *You'll be sorry, bitch.*

She became hysterical and he sat her on the bed to calm her down. She buried her face in his chest. Without meaning to he began to stroke her hair. Suddenly she put both arms around his neck and kissed him fiercely and his hand strayed under her shirt. She was tearing at his clothes and he found himself on top of her. She put him in, almost roughly, and he lay there for a moment, motionless, feeling for the first time subsumed, complete. Then she began moving under him, slow circular motions, and instinctively he tensed his legs and pointed his toes. He felt his nose, lips, his entire face suffuse with blood. Little currents of pleasure flowed down his legs from the root to the very ends of his toes. It was all he could do to stop himself from coming and when he did, he shuddered and stopped, shuddered and stopped many times over. When it truly was over, she took his finger and put it at the exact spot so he could return the favour.

'Stay with me,' she whispered, 'I'm afraid.'

He lay there a long time, thinking with almost mystic calm, this is what I've been missing all my life.

But all she could think in her turn was, It didn't take long to replace you, did it, Tariq? And the thing is, I don't even know his name.

5

Piyumi's mother called.

'I've booked you on the Colombo flight next Tuesday.'

'But that's in a week!' She didn't dare mention her misfortunes. Her mother would have said, 'What do you expect, living in Brixton?' You didn't get rogue boyfriends going around trashing flats in Knightsbridge.

Not according to her.

'Have you made a start on your packing?'

'Actually, the stuff is all out of the cupboards.'

It was all over the floor, down the corridor, in the kitchen. Tariq had even flung some of her clothes into the bath.

'Have you stopped the milk?'

'No, but I stopped the boyfriend.'

'What's that?'

'Nothing.'

'You really must learn not to mumble, dear.'

At work she said: 'My flat's been broken into. I need time to sort it all out.'

They were only too glad to give her leave.

Marek didn't have her number. In the evenings the buzzer

rang and rang, but she ignored it. Once he must have got into the flats when someone else was entering. There was a note pushed under her door, hurt and petulant. It just said:

'Why are you doing this to me?'

She didn't want to see Marek. I've had enough of men for the moment, she thought. My life is too full of selfish men, and a mother who might as well have been a man for all the comfort she gives me. I have lived my life too long on hard chairs. I need something soft to sink back into, something old and shabby. A different country.

Marek was one of those things that just happened. One of those things you do without thinking. A half-a-night stand. Anyway, he got more out of it than I did. I gave him good value for money. She was shocked by the boldness of this thought even as she thought it.

Marek walked into the grey office block next to a grey Registry Office on a grey London street. There were two other candidates in the waiting room: a nice middle-aged lady in blue overalls who sat knitting; and a young man, thin and pinched and Asian, who said, 'I have a PhD from the University of Oxford Street. I have ACBT and CIMA. I speak Welsh fluently.' Marek wondered whether he should turn round and walk out, as he had done at other interviews. Just then an oldish Englishman came out. He had disconcertingly orange hair.

'Mr Marek Markovic? I'll see you now.'

Inside there was a large map on the wall, green, with lots of yellow near the top and brown in the middle.

'My name is Percy ffinch-Percy,' he said. 'Do sit down.'

Marek sat. Mr ffinch-Percy pulled out a long steel pointer and began to point at the map. You could tell that somewhere in his past life he had been a geography teacher.

'Do you know where this is?'

Marek shook his head.

'The island of Sri Lanka. The teardrop in the Indian Ocean. A misnomer if ever there was one. Nobody cries over there. They lost the capacity a long time ago.'

He jabbed at a point somewhere near the bottom on the left. 'This is Colombo, the capital city. Home to the Mogambo International School. Small, exclusive.' He sucked in air through his teeth and puffed out his chest. '. . . of which I'm headmaster. For my sins.' He giggled. 'You have a degree in history, I believe?'

Marek nodded.

'But how is your math?'

'I barely got through O level,' Marek replied ruefully.

'Excellent, excellent. Perhaps we can try you in the sixth form then. What about your French?'

Marek shook his head. 'Don't speak a word, I'm afraid.'

'Neither did the last French teacher,' said Mr ffinch-Percy sadly. Then he brightened up. 'How good are you with computers?'

'Totally alien to me.'

'That's a great shame. At the moment we've put Fernando

in charge of ICT. Now there's no one to open the gates.'
He passed for a moment thinking. 'Of course we could hire
Mr Desai.' He pointed to the waiting room outside and his
voice fell to a conspiratorial whisper. 'Tremendously over-
qualified, but keeps coming back for interviews. Won't do at
all, I'm afraid. Wrong skin colour.'

Marek looked shocked.

'Oh, it's not us,' said Mr ffinch-Percy. 'We're not the racists
here. It's the Sri Lankan parents, you see. If they're paying
good money to have their kiddies taught at an International
School, the very least they can expect and demand is a few
white faces on the staff.' He got up, signifying the interview
was at end. 'We'll be in touch. You can send in Mrs Mulhern
now.'

Marek went up to Mrs Mulhern. 'You're next,' he said.
'Good luck!'

Mrs Mulhern looked up from her knitting, startled.
'Oh, I'm not here for the job, dear. I'm here to clean up after
Mr Percy's finished. Makes an awful mess, Mr Percy does.'

Outside, all Marek could think of was Piyumi. Call me, he
kept willing her silently. Call me! He cursed himself for not
having taken her number when he crept out that morning.

He went to see Mr Skanda, the one sure way of getting
through to her.

'That girl you were with the other day. Has she been in?
Do you have her number?'

'Girl? What girl? Mr Skanda looked puzzled. He didn't
seem to have any recollection of that last meeting on
the stairway.

'Outside my flat,' Marek said desperately. 'Below yours.'

Mr Skanda thought about it for a bit. 'There's plenty of guava juice,' he said. 'Just arrived.'

Marek went back, for what must have been the twentieth time, to Triangle Place. For a council block of flats it looked strangely deserted. No one went in, no one came out.

'Piyumi!' he shouted, feeling very self-conscious as he did. His voice echoed round the red-brick triangular court. 'Piyumi!'

No answer. No one even bothered to throw open a window and tell him to shut up. After a while he went home.

At nine o'clock next morning the phone rang. Marek leapt out of bed to get it. She was in more trouble, he thought. Just like her to call only when she needed help.

'About time too!' he yelled.

'Well, I've been as quick as I could,' said Mr ffinch-Percy. 'It wasn't an easy decision to make, I assure you. But you've got the job.'

Marek didn't know whether to laugh or cry. 'You don't seem very excited,' Mr ffinch-Percy said.

'I am,' he assured him, 'I am.'

'Only one thing, though. You have to take up the position next week.'

'Next week?'

'There are plenty of other people if you don't want the job,' said Percy ffinch-Percy. (Marek had a vision of Mrs Mulhern in front of the class. 'Now, children,' she said, waving her needles.) 'I need an answer by this afternoon. If you accept, you can come in tomorrow and sign the papers. I myself have to catch the flight back tomorrow night, you see.'

And so it happened that Piyumi and Marek rediscovered each other in the queue for the Colombo flight the following Tuesday. The kaleidoscope had turned, the little scraps of blue and red and gold juxtaposed in a pretty pattern. You could almost call it serendipity.

'You could have rung,' he said accusingly.

'I'm sorry,' she replied. She didn't really mean it. Nevertheless they sat next to each other on the plane. She fell asleep with her head on his shoulder, and he had an erection all the way to Colombo. He had to hobble off the plane at the other end.

Viraj drove his sparkling yellow tuk-tuk through Deal Place, the short cut to the gym. He had money in his pocket and his hair looked great (as indeed it should after an hour or so of preparation). His armpits were freshly shaved, the baby oil on his muscles gleamed. Definition, definition, definition! The mantra of every body-builder. It was rather like location, location, location, really. Finishing the last of his Body-Plus, he flicked the carton into a passing garden where it hit Mr Herath on the head.

Mr Herath was in the front garden planting sweet potatoes. ('Sweet potatoes only encourage rats,' said Mrs Herath. 'Oh rats!' said Mr Herath.) Mr Herath wasn't used to being hit on the head by empty cartons of Body-Plus, but it was one of the hazards of having a low garden wall in Colombo. He looked up to see a muscular torso in a white banian and white tracksuit bottoms driving past in a three-wheeler.

One of the most gratifying parts of a visit to the gym was your entrance. Viraj stood on the threshold for a second, posing. Everyone looked at him, and immediately looked away with studied indifference. Bingo! He knew he looked good, man, really good.

Debs was setting up the bench press and he sauntered over to help.

'Machang!' He clapped her on the back.

'Machang!' Her Sinhala was getting good. Better still, she spoke it like a man.

She lay on the bench and he climbed onto the metal pads on either side of her prone body. There was a little runnel of sweat trickling between her breasts. There was also a tattoo just there, in the shape of a sword. On the handle it said 'Angela'.

She raised her sturdy brown arms to receive the bar from him and he admired the little blond tufts of hair in her armpits. (He liked that in a woman.) He hoped she was enjoying the view up. One of his great dreams, as yet unrealized, was to wake up in the morning to find Debs on top, riding him hard and mercilessly, and him begging her to stop. She wouldn't, of course, and they would finally fall back spent and exhausted.

'Hard night?'

She nodded, moving the wad of chewing gum from one side of her mouth to the other. 'I went to Colombo 2000 with the guys from work.' Debs worked for an NGO which was so well organized and delegated (she said) it left her plenty of time. Most afternoons she was in the gym.

'And you?'

Viraj shook his head. He couldn't afford nights out. Even if he'd had the money, he was too tired most nights. What money he earned he kept for Body-Plus and hair products. His elderly, uncomplaining parents had plundered their savings to buy him a three-wheeler on hire purchase, brand new and sparkling yellow, on which he paid a daily 250 rupees earned from hires. In the meantime they fed and housed him—it was their duty after all: he was the prize stallion that would one day romp home with the Gold Cup, marrying the pretty girl with the fat dowry. That was the way all Sinhala teledramas ended, and life was nothing if not a Sinhala teledrama.

But there was time enough for that. You didn't get married till you were old and fat and not much good for anything else. In the meantime, there was Debs. He longed for her to scoop him up in her strong arms and take him off to Holland where she came from. The visa officers, the border police, the immigration officials, all would fall senseless at her approach. All gates would be flung open.

Viraj somehow knew it wouldn't quite happen like that, but there was no harm in dreaming. Abroad was that Great Golden Land out there that every Sri Lankan considers his natural birthright. For the princely sum of 50,000 rupees his neighbour had even promised to deliver the visa to his door. Where was he to find 50,000? Imported hair products were so expensive these days!

But things were about to change. Last evening on his way back from work he had met his neighbour, L.M. Siddhu, at the Matara Tea Rooms.

'What we need,' said L.M. Siddhu, 'is a nice, personable young man such as yourself to be our agent. I represent a very rich client, let's call him Mr X, who wishes to remain anonymous. In order to effect all his philanthropy he needs people on the ground, people who can run around, people who are not ashamed to get their hands dirty. You do speak good Sinhala, don't you?'

Viraj nodded.

'There'll be certain foreign friends of Mr X arriving—Sri Lankan expats—and we'll be needing you to facilitate their stay. You can do that, can't you?'

Viraj nodded.

'By the way, here's 2500 rupees. Consider it as a sort of advance on future work. On the days you work for us we will, of course, take care of the payment on your three-wheeler.'

Two weeks' supply of Body-Plus! Things were definitely looking up.

6

It was pol sambal for dinner again.

'I've left the bandakka for tomorrow's lunch,' said Mrs Herath.

It was not that the Heraths disliked pol sambal—on the contrary, the possibility of fresh pol sambal for dinner had been one of the main planks of their retirement policy, what had kept them going through all the years of slaving away in London. But it was galling to eat it two nights in a row; especially when there was fresh asparagus on sale from Nuwara Eliya at Food City, and they couldn't afford it.

They'd had it all worked out. The sterling pension was more than enough to cover every eventuality. But inflation was running riot and unaccountably, the rupee was getting stronger.

'I know what we should do,' said Mrs Herath. 'Let's rent out the spare bedroom.'

'Bollocks,' said Mr Herath.

'I heard that,' said Mrs Herath.

Finally, he came round to the idea. 'Only, no locals,' he warned.

'No locals,' she agreed.

Sri Lankan tenancy laws were so weighted against landlords that no one wanted to let out rooms to locals. You couldn't get them out. As a result, Sri Lankan tenants found it very difficult to get decent accommodation, the very law that was supposed to help working against them.

The Heraths called in a couple of brokers, prosperous-looking women in kurtas and vast quantities of gold jewellery.

Only foreigners, they were warned.

'I have an excellent tenant,' said one. 'A Nigerian national.'

'Just arrived?'

'He's been here quite a while, actually. In Magazine Road, Borella.'

'Oh? Why is he moving?'

'He's being released. Can you imagine, they found half a kilo of heroin on him at the airport! His so-called friend made him carry it, of course.'

'Of course.'

The second broker shook her head. 'Very difficult to get foreigners these days. These bombs are chasing them all away. But you know what, my son will be back from the UK soon. He's looking for a room.'

'Is he English?'

'No, but he's quite fair.'

'Thanks,' said Mr Herath, 'but no thanks.'

'He's got a degree from Oxford Street College,' said the broker defensively. 'ACBT, CIMA.'

'Excellent,' said Mr Herath. 'Now get out!'

The Heraths were consoling each other on their front

verandah when the answer to all their troubles walked past, small and gingery, but unmistakably white: Percy ffinch-Percy. They had seen him around these last couple of days. He lived in a chummery up the road, a house full of young men.

'Yoo-hoo!' shouted Mrs Herath, trotting out to collar him. 'We want you to come live with us.'

This impromptu invitation was not as unusual as it might sound. It was a favourite sport in Colombo, poaching your neighbour's tenants. Indeed, in certain parts of Colpetty it was open season on foreigners. You didn't covet your neighbour's wife —so boring, so biblical!—you coveted his tenants. Far more satisfying and besides, you saved the month's brokerage. Mr ffinch-Percy for his part was not unused to these unsolicited advances. In his time in Sri Lanka he had been propositioned by all sorts of people: three-wheeler kariars, shopkeepers, even schoolboys. This was the first time a little old lady had thrown herself at him. She wasn't what you'd call hot; but then to be perfectly fair, neither was he.

They dragged him in and showed him the spare room. 'Ooh, a double bed!' he giggled. 'But you know, I'm perfectly happy where I am.'

'You'll be getting good home-cooked food,' threatened Mrs Herath. 'Garden produce.'

'I may have just the person for you,' said Percy ffinch-Percy.

From the phone on the wall behind the aged freezer cabinet, Mr Skanda put through a call.

'The eagle has landed,' he said to the person at the other end.

It was all so very like a 1970s film.

They stepped off the plane into a wall of water. Piyumi had forgotten that all-encompassing, all-pervading miasma of wetness, diluted with the aromas of dry fish and copra. She breathed in deeply and, like a plant long deprived of water whose tendrils begin to uncurl, felt the faintest stirrings of life in her limbs. The traffic was much worse than she remembered. There were huge cut-outs of politicians along the route, oversized in their magnificence, advertising the forthcoming elections. Her Uncle Bala was at the airport to meet her in the ancient harvest gold Toyota Crown, one of twelve imported by Mrs Bandaranaike in the 1970s for the first Non-Aligned Conference, to ferry heads of state about. It was still running, though in a non-aligned sort of way.

'Where are they putting you up?' she asked Marek.

'Somewhere called Deal Place.'

'That's in Colpetty,' Uncle Bala said. 'We can drop you off.' They were met at the gates of the chummery by Mr ffinch-Percy.

'Welcome,' he said with his sticky-sweet smile, 'welcome!'

Uncle Bala insisted on bringing Marek's stuff in so they all trooped in to have a look. At a round table by the window were two male students.

'I give them a lot of tuition,' explained Mr ffinch-Percy. 'You'd be surprised how keen they are to learn.' He looked fondly at them. They were chattering to each other, oblivious to the guests. They also appeared to be giving each other a manicure.

'Must be this New Math they keep talking about,' muttered Uncle Bala.

'Boys!' Mr ffinch-Percy clapped his hands. 'Boys! Go upstairs and practise your logarithms.' Twittering and complaining they left, one of them sticking his tongue out at ffinch-Percy behind his back.

'Phew, that's better. Now Marek, I've fixed you up with a lovely couple just up the road. Much more peaceful there than in this, this henhouse. And home-cooked food, you lucky bugger.' He dug Marek in the ribs.

So they all trooped up the road and dropped Marek at the Heraths' door.

'You'll call me, won't you?' Marek asked Piyumi desperately. What he meant was, Don't leave me, please!

'Of course,' said Piyumi.

7

Aunty Chelvam's house was of a beauty so luminous, so incandescent, it left you breathless. The classical perfection of its tall white columns of polished chunam, its broken pediments, its bottled balustrades, was tempered with just that touch of Arts and Crafts to prevent it from sterility. It rose, shimmering like a wraith, out of a sea of tropical flowering hardwoods, cassia and jacaranda and tulip.

'Let me out here,' said Piyumi at the gates. 'I want to walk.'

If architecture were truly frozen music, then this was perhaps Mozart's twenty-first piano concerto. Or maybe, she thought whimsically, Roberta Flack singing 'The First Time Ever I Saw Your Face'. She knew she ought to have trained as an architect. Law, for all the subtlety of its arcane logic and the sinuous reasoning of its argument, never allowed for the sheer physical presence of beauty: that living breathing thing you could hold in your hands, turn over, sniff and take a bite out of. For her a good building was just that: something good enough to eat.

Piyumi's great-grandfather had built it at the turn of the

century in Cinnamon Gardens, that new area of Colombo people had begun moving to when the soot and grime of coaling ships had made the old areas near the port uninhabitable. As tradition demanded, he had left it in its entirety to his youngest, Aunty Chelvam. There were seven descendants now, scattered all over the world, waiting at the take-away counter for their share of the pie to keep them in the suburban splendour to which they had become accustomed in the West.

'Demolish! Demolish!' they clamoured with the cunning of those who were quite sure they knew the value of money. Piyumi was heart-broken. Was she the only one who placed a value on it beyond price? Didn't it mean anything that her ancestor had sat down with a draughtsman for days, poring over plans? That he had tramped from tree to tree on his snake-ridden estates to select the best timber for the roof? That was how you did things those days. In the East, where codes of behaviour were so rigid, so stylized, a house was a purer expression of the self than almost anything else: it spelt out the subtext of your life far more clearly than your behaviour ever could. Her great-grandfather had built it: it was a hologram of his memory, a blueprint of his genes.

And finally, he had given it that all-important name without which no house those days was complete. He had called it Serendipity.

You might have expected Piyumi's aunts, uncles and cousins to be aware of this, but they were indifferent.

'What I'd really like,' said Aunty Pushpam that evening at the family conference, 'is for all of us to get together and build a lovely modern block of flats, all air-conditioned. We can each have one. They allow you six floors in this area. I checked.'

'No good,' said cousin Dhanu, he of the chewing gum, tattoos and shaved head. As well as himself, Dhanu represented two elderly cousins, both living in Florida. He himself lived in deepest Alabama with his girlfriend LaToya, whose picture he would show you upon the slightest provocation. 'LaToya and I are getting married in spring. We need the apartment over there, not here, I'm afraid.'

'We won't get much for the land,' said Uncle Bala. Piyumi realized he was the only one who might be recruited as a possible ally. He turned to her. 'The government is fighting two wars, one against the Tigers in the north, the other a much more insidious one against the Marxist JVP in the south. You'd be a fool to want to invest in land in this climate.'

'I hear the JVP have threatened to cut off your ears if they catch you listening to Beethoven.'

'Wouldn't have mattered to Beethoven. He was deaf anyway.'

'Does anyone know,' asked Aunty Pushpam, 'did Van Gogh compose any music?'

Piyumi listened to this conversation as it steered its dangerous course between the twin rocks of the Tigers and the JVP. She thought of Mr Skanda. 'Call me once a week,' he had said, 'Wednesday evenings before my meeting.'

Every once in a while the talk came back to the much more important family matter at hand. Absolutely nobody else wanted to keep the house. Piyumi ate her way silently through the pumpkin soup, the fish moulee, the crème caramel: because cooks in these Colombo Seven houses still worked to the age-old dictum of Eastern for lunch, Western for dinner. Though even she had to admit it was somewhat better than Knightsbridge. Not much. Somewhat.

Marek had a sleepless night.

'We've got you the best Ceyesta mattress,' said Mrs Herath proudly.

It was strung so tight it was like a very firmly packed sack of potatoes. The fan overhead, a shiny black thing that looked remarkably like the propeller of a B-12 bomber, was governed not by a regulator, but a switch. When you put it on, the whole room vibrated in preparation for lift-off. Marek had visions of it flying off the ceiling and chopping him up into very small bits. The Heraths would find him next morning not merely resting in peace but resting in pieces.

He tried turning it off. The mosquitoes invaded the room and bit him alive. He turned it back on. The sheer terror of it was too much. Towards morning he drifted off into a nightmarish stupor from which he was woken by Mrs Herath with a very weak cup of tea. Percy ffinch-Percy was waiting for him in the sitting room.

'Chop, chop!' he said with his sticky-sweet smile. 'We have school to teach.'

In London, Marek's mother sat at the pitch-pine kitchen table with Dennis Ridoynauth from downstairs. They were halfway through a bottle of Lambrusco. Full-bodied, yet sweet and bubbly. Rather like me, she thought.

'My drum beats only for you,' said Mr Ridoynauth attempting to take her hand.

'Then please make it stop. I have a headache.'

The phone rang. 'Hi, Ma, it's me.' She didn't say anything. 'Are you okay there?'

'Fine,' she said suspiciously. 'Why shouldn't I be?'

'I'm sorry I left in such a hurry.'

'You do what you have to do.' There was an edge of steel to her voice. 'You know I'm the last person to stop you.'

'It's only for a year. I'll be back before you know it.'

'Whether I'll be here is a different matter.' She laughed throatily.

The Mogambo International was housed in a rather ugly fifties' dwelling in a leafy side street of Colombo Seven, not far from Serendipity. There were just fifteen children in Marek's history class, more girls than boys. The girls were all eighteen going on thirty-eight. They wore short (very short) black skirts and black nail polish. The Mogambo International had no school uniform—'We believe a uniform constricts the mind', said Mr ffinch-Percy—but they might as well have had one: black skirts and black nail polish. There were only five boys in the class, including Princy whom Marek recognized from the chummery. He too wore black nail polish. They were all enormously interested in Marek.

'Please, sir, do you have a girlfriend, sir?'

'Please, sir, do you have a mistress, sir?'

'In that case, sir, do you have a mister, sir?'

'Do you have any friends at all, sir?'

'So what are you doing out here then, sir?'

Marek put up his arms to fend off these questions which were like blows to the head.

'That's for me to know and you to find out. Tell me what other A Levels you're doing,' he said, changing the subject.

'Mr Fernando teaches me ICT,' said Iresha. She wore the shortest skirt of all. Marek's eyes kept straying to her plump thighs which she crossed and re-crossed with alarming regularity. 'I've just finished teaching him how to twitter.'

'Please, sir, Iresha will teach you anything you want. She teaches all the masters, sir.'

'Oh, shut up, Princy! Please, sir, Princy goes to Mr ffinch-Percy for Gay Levels, sir. They're up all night doing practicals.'

The whole class erupted. At this point ffinch-Percy walked in. Behind him was a demure girl in plaits and the white school uniform of a government school.

'Children, children!' He waited for the noise to subside. 'I want to introduce you to Somawathie who'll be joining you from today.'

The whole class went quiet as they scrutinized the new arrival, who looked coyly from side to side through lowered eyes. Her arrival took the heat off Marek, who was able to continue teaching after that without incident. By the end of the morning he had learnt that Iresha's father was in the timber business. Princy's parents lived on a tea estate up-country. He stayed at the chummery on weekdays, going up only at weekends.

'Please, sir, you need a haircut, sir. Princy can cut it for you. He can perm it, he can colour it, he can do anything you like. You should see what he's done to Mr ffinch-Percy's hair.'

'I have,' said Marek in awed tones.

'Don't listen to her, sir, she's just jealous.'

'Bitch!'

'Double bitch!'

At the end of classes, two men in army fatigues and submachine guns came to escort Somawathie out.

'Who is she?' Marek asked curiously.

'Oh, no one special. I think her father's the leader of the opposition or something.'

Iresha followed him out. 'I could show you round,' she said hopefully, 'introduce you to some nice people, maybe. There's a preview at Barefoot Wednesday evening.'

Marek smiled at her. 'Thanks,' he said. 'We'll see.'

He crossed the road. Parked under an enormous mara tree, with branches as high as a cathedral roof, was a three-wheeler, brand new and sparkling yellow. It had flashing lights on its roof, red and blue, which spelled out the word Amma. The driver threw away a carton of something he was drinking and sprang to attention when he saw Marek.

'Where you go?' he asked.

'I'm looking for Serendipity,' Marek replied. Which was ironic, really, because serendipity was usually something you only encountered when you least expected it.

8

The prospective owners of Serendipity, Bala and Pushpam, Dhanu, Piyumi, and ancient Aunty Ganga all piled into the Toyota Crown, and headed off to the offices of Bilious and Dicey in the Fort.

They arrived at the wrong floor by mistake to be greeted by a rather jovial white woman with very well-defined biceps.

'Bilious? Next floor up. We're Women in Want here.' She pointed to a board half hidden behind a rather dusty rubber plant, which proclaimed 'Women in Want'.

'I am always in want of a woman,' muttered Bala, 'though she's not exactly the sort of woman I had in mind.' Aunty Pushpam gave him a dirty look.

After the motley crew of people left the office, Debs sat transfixed, smitten. She wanted to run out after them shouting: 'Can I take you out for a drink? The White Horse, perhaps? The Blue Elephant? The Pink Sheep? Can I take down your number? Can I take down your skirt?' But she was a suddhi, a white woman, and the dignity of her position forbade it. What would the rest of her Sri Lankan staff think?

The object of her desire was at that moment sitting directly overhead, quarrelling gently with her relatives: Piyumi.

On the next floor they met Mr Sinnetambe, their lawyer.

'The land has been surveyed, the seven sub-divisions approved, with a common roadway to the plots at the back.' He rustled the papers on his desk. 'My advice to you, however, is to sell the whole block. Put your money where it can't be touched. There's this very sound company at the moment called Golden Key which is giving thirty per cent.'

In the back of everybody's mind were the riots of 1983 when buildings had been torched and people driven out of their homes. Many had disposed of their assets at forced-sale prices. Better to sell when you could actually get a fair market price.

'My mother and I want to keep our piece,' said Piyumi. She was as much shocked by the sound of her voice as they were.

'Your mother doesn't come into it,' said Ganga sharply. 'It comes to you directly from your father.'

This was actually just as well: although Piyumi didn't tell them this, her mother, too, would have been in an unholy hurry to sell. Like many of her generation, her mother had lived through too many of the vicissitudes of history to have any faith in the power of landholding, the romance of ownership. Better to keep your money in stocks and bonds, gold and jewels, little things you could hide easily from the mob when the time came.

'I don't want to sell my share.' They all looked at her in disbelief.

'Outrageous,' muttered Uncle Bala.

'I can't believe you're doing this to us,' said Dhanu. 'Without your piece we're left with an irregular block no developer will want. You're devaluing our land.'

'And you're devaluing mine!' Piyumi shot back. 'How will I be able to live in my servants' quarters with your tower block looming over it?'

Piyumi living in the servants' quarters? Shock and horror contorted their faces.

'I always said there was bad blood on the mother's side,' said Ganga dangerously.

They drove back in silence. Piyumi was quite surprised they didn't ask her to get out and walk.

Serendipity had originally been designed to be run by a staff of about fifteen people. In Aunty Chelvam's day there had been two upstairs boys who were entrusted to do the bedrooms, and two downstairs for the reception rooms. There was a woman lavatory coolie in a knee-length sari whose sole job it was to keep the bathrooms clean. This she did on a daily basis by sloshing copious amounts of water around the floor and walls so the bathroom had barely enough time to dry before she began again next day. She didn't live in. She arrived every day, mid-morning, did her rounds, was fed in the servants' kitchen and departed before five, where to, nobody knew. You came to realize the flood-level sari was a badge of office almost, wet knees being an occupational hazard. The water in the bathroom drained into a small hole in the corner, through which, every night, arrived delegations of friendly cockroaches the size of chocolate digestives. This wildlife-in-the-wetlands was one aspect of tropical living that left Piyumi trembling.

Then there was the garden: the province of the head gardener, his assistant, and the garden boy, a stick-thin brown child of twelve who sang in high clear notes like a bird. His job was basically to do all the work while the other two quarrelled over the aesthetic composition of various flowerbeds, or whether it was better to prune the flamboyant before the rains or after, or whether the recent spate of bad luck on the house of Segarajasingham had been brought about by the Queen of the Night being planted too close to the house. The garden boy wasn't really interested in aesthetics. What he mostly wanted to do was sleep. He could do this virtually anywhere, even standing up, while the arguments raged back and forth over his head about which bit of lawn he should mow first. But his favourite place was under the tabeubia, the pale pink blossoms falling softly on him while he slept, turning him into a sort of tender, tropical flower child.

The kitchens were the fiefdom of the cook and the cook's cook. The cook managed the food of the house, those various nursery dishes so beloved of memsahibs and Sri Lankans of a certain class: the mulligatawny, the beef olives, the rhubarb crumble. The cook's cook fed the staff on a far more austere diet of unpolished red rice, dried sprats, fresh sardines and anchovies; the bigger fish like tuna and seer and marlin being reserved for the big house. When it was found years later that mercury levels were higher in the big fish, Uncle Bala exclaimed: 'No wonder they were all so sane and we were all so mad!' To round off the numbers there was a live-in handyman on permanent standby; and a night watchman instructed to ring his bell loudly every half hour so you could rest easy, secure in the knowledge he was on the job. What he did instead was to give everyone a thoroughly sleepless night.

Last but not least there were two drivers, his and hers, because Piyumi's great-grandmother was a full head taller than her great-grandfather, and preferred to arrive separately at any function. It was a question of aesthetics once again.

All this was much changed now. There was now a single cook at Serendipity. Then there was Suranganee, who managed pretty much everything else. Suranganee, a force of nature, a force majeure. If you wanted the light bulb in your bedroom changed or the clothes on the line brought in because it was going to rain, or quite simply an extra teaspoon of sugar in your tea, it was Suranganee you called. There were three Segarajasinghams in the house apart from Piyumi: it never occurred to any of them that they could do this work themselves.

Suranganee was conversant in all three languages: Sinhalese by birth, she spoke Tamil tolerably, as many did who were born upcountry. Her English was fluent but atrocious, with an accent that defied all description. She had no formal education whatsoever, but was qualified for a PhD at least in telephony. She was a master of the instrument.

When the phone rang, Suranganee was invariably the first to reach it. If you were the caller and she didn't like you, she simply hung up. If you tried again she told you there was no one at home. Aunty Pushpam who was quite slow on the uptake hovered in vain while Suranganee held on to the phone with an iron fist. 'No,' Suranganee would say into it, 'there's absolutely no one else here.'

'Who's that?' Aunty Pushpam asked.

'Who's that?' the caller asked, hearing Aunty Pushpam in the background.

'Oh, it's only the dog.'

'Dog?' Aunty Pushpam asked wonderingly. 'We don't have a dog.'

Suranganee put a hand over the receiver. 'It's someone from the municipality. They want to know if have we vaccinated our dog against rabies.'

This was Suranganee, who ruled their lives.

Viraj dropped Marek at the gates to Serendipity, cheerfully fleecing him of 500 rupees. I wonder what sort of people live in a place like this, Viraj thought. All the several hundred inhabitants of the colony he lived in, his watte, would have fitted comfortably within its grounds. He couldn't help noticing Suranganee who opened the gates, her pert breasts jiggling unrestrictedly inside the thin pink dress. Then reality took hold. Nah, he said to himself, Debs is the only woman for me.

From her upstairs bedroom window, Piyumi watched

Marek come up the drive. She wondered what Suranganee would make of this strange suddha, this white man. Suranganee would show him into the best reception room, of course, the one reserved for visiting dignitaries. (A suddha, any suddha, was a dignitary even if he happened to be a convicted paedophile with weeping sores.)

Let him wait ten minutes, she thought. That's how things are done at Serendipity. The house was beginning to work its archaic charms on her: she was beginning to feel not a little feudal herself. When she came down, Marek was looking at the black and white photographs on the piano. (Prince Philip with Uncle Bala and Aunty Pushpam, she in zebra-striped fifties' sunglasses looking ineffably cool; Aunty Chelvam at the Vatican, uncharacteristically veiled and pious. She was to ditch both husband and religion four months after the photograph.)

'Hi!'

'Hi!'

She looked so fresh, so poised, so in control of her surroundings. They lied, whoever said the picture doesn't change with the frame, he thought. For the first time he could see what she meant, the meaning of her. Her meaning didn't lie among the red-brick council blocks of Brixton. It lay here.

'Let me show you my inheritance,' she said. She led him through the arch under the stairs and out into the back garden. There had once been fifteen rooms here—the servants' quarters—all in a row. Over the years the middle had been demolished, leaving two square Palladian pavilions at either end with pyramidal roofs and a stretch of lawn in between.

'Mine's the one to the left.'

They inspected the great triangular timber trusses that held up the roof, the eighteen-inch walls of cabook now bulging in places, the window openings barred and shuttered. 'A good lick of paint and I'm moving in,' she said.

He looked at her, a sudden idea forming in his head. 'I'll do it. I'll paint it for you. All my life I've worked as a painter on building sites.'

She hesitated. He could see the doubts scudding across her mind like black clouds.

'You don't have to pay me. I won't expect anything in return.'

Still she hesitated. Then she took his hand and squeezed it, and smiled. He smiled back. But in his mind he was shouting for joy: No you don't have to pay me at all. Just fuck me! Fuck me! Fuck me!

They went to Lanley's for the paint. ('Any colour as long as it's white,' she said.) He persuaded her to paint the window shutters and bars a blue-green colour by scraping away the old layers of paint and showing her the original colour underneath: blue-green.

The other inhabitants of the house came one by one to watch this strange suddha at work. They couldn't quite believe Piyumi would move in when it was ready: she had no idea what she was letting herself in for.

'The Sri Lanka of today is not what you left as a child,' Aunty Pushpam said wistfully. 'A country is like a river. It moves on whether you're there or not. You can never step into the same river twice.'

'What sort of defeatist attitude is that?'

'This idea of saving Serendipity. You're being hopelessly romantic, that's all I'm saying.'

'A country is the sum total of its million and one individual parts,' Piyumi said. 'I am one of those. If I choose to be hopelessly romantic, I am, in some small way, helping to redefine its meaning.'

'It's not yours to redefine. You forfeited that right when you left.'

'Is that what you really think?' Piyumi's eyes flashed dangerously. 'That this is only for the likes of you, safe in your Colombo Seven houses, who've done nothing for our people out there, the injustices they've had to face because you kept your mouth shut?'

'Our people? Correct me if I'm wrong. Don't you have that wonderful little thing called a British passport? How does that make you our people?'

Piyumi was silent.

'There is a sort of system here . . .' Aunty Pushpam said quietly. 'You live inside it. You don't change it from outside. Any change has to come from within.'

'Watch me,' Piyumi said. 'Just watch me.'

9

Marek entered the crowded cobbled courtyard of Barefoot behind Iresha, in the wake of her softly undulating creamy thighs. They were an easy act to follow, he thought, watching the silver sheath dress she wore barely skimming the tops of them. She led him past a large wooden statue of a bull on two legs wearing a headdress.

'This is what we call rent-a-crowd,' she said.

They were there to view the work of a famous artist, a thin, wasted young man with a ponytail. He had an unhealthy pallor to his cheeks as if he had spent the last few years in a bunker, surfacing only now to exhibit his wares. Every now and then he made hopeless little forays into the crush to try and drag unsuspecting individuals back into the exhibition room: an uphill task.

Looking around at guests upholstered in their finest, under the soft pools of light among the trees, Marek fancifully imagined he was deep inside the belly of some monstrous bejewelled beast, masticating its food, swishing its tail from side to side, preening itself from every angle. It seemed to him that the rent-a-crowd was interested in only one thing: itself.

It came to these functions to meet: itself. It was only interested in one opinion: its own. It flickered its lazy dragon eye briefly over the art, trying to decide whether it was worth it or not, while the artist quivered in anticipation. If he was worth the trouble he was instantly consumed, subsumed. But his acceptance was also his death: no art could survive the gastric juices of this prehensile animal.

'What I have tried to express here, and I don't know if I've succeeded or not,' the artist coughed delicately, 'is that all art springs from the earth itself, the very fountainhead of creation.'

The work was a hideously realistic phallus, ten times life-size, fashioned in clay.

'Bet you had fun with it, though,' said Percy ffinch-Percy, winking and nudging the artist in the ribs. 'Did you work from life?'

'I never work from life,' the artist explained patiently. 'Life is incorrect. Life is disappointing. It is only in my mind that I find the perfection I seek.'

'I always work from life,' said Princy. 'What's a little disappointment between friends?'

They moved on to the next exhibit, an even bigger representation of the female parts.

There was a kerfuffle at the door as two army types walked in, followed by a woman in a striped silk sari. (That one! said Maleeshya of *Chi! Magazine* and instantly the bulbs flashed and the photographer took six pictures in quick succession.) The woman had black oiled hair piled high on her head into which she had stuck two jewelled kuru, like knitting needles. In her hand was a cane receptacle rather like a birdcage.

'Looks like she's just walked off the set of *The Mikado*,' sniggered Iresha.

Around her neck Marek could see an aquamarine the size of a golf ball.

'Just because they own the mines.'

Marek didn't say anything. The transformation from schoolgirl to woman was complete, and he thought Somawathie looked rather nice actually.

Debs spotted Piyumi immediately. She bore down on her, with her man-sized hands outstretched.

'You don't know me but I know you. You came into my office the other day looking for Bilious. You see, I am "Woman in Want".'

The hot breath of her desire enveloped Piyumi, crackling around her like a California bush fire.

'Let me buy you a drink. I want to get to know you better.'

She found herself being propelled to the bar past myriad Sri Lankan faces she would much rather have got to know.

'Why is it,' she wondered hopelessly, 'that only white people find me attractive?'

Outside in the car park, the security guard told Viraj to turn his music down. The Bollywood Bhangra of his tuk-tuk didn't sit well with the cool jazz emanating from the courtyard. He watched his lights change from red to blue to red while he waited for his woman to finish. Whatever time of day or night, he didn't consider his work done till he'd dropped her home. She never asked him in: but he lived in hope. Till then, the firm handshake, the manly hug on the doorstep—that was enough.

And so the animal that was rent-a-crowd brayed on into the night, oblivious to everything but itself, oblivious certainly to the young man in the exhibition room with the unsold body parts; till the last glass of headache-inducing wine had been drunk to the dregs, the last asparagus roll squashed firmly underfoot; and it was time to go home.

From Serendipity, Piyumi dialled Mr Skanda. 'I'm just back from Barefoot.'

'Tell me,' he said. 'Tell me about the intelligentsia. Tell me about the bourgeoisie.'

'Such long words, Mr Skanda. I never heard you use such long words before!'

But Mr Skanda was not about to rise to her coquetry. 'Tell me,' he said. 'If there were to be . . .' he paused, choosing his words carefully, 'some sort of disturbance . . .'

'Disturbance? What disturbance?' she asked suspiciously. 'I didn't know charities got themselves involved in disturbances.'

'Oh, it's nothing like that, I assure you. I mean if there was some civil unrest, perhaps . . . and the army were called in to quell it. Whose side would the intelligentsia take?'

'That's easy. The underdog, Mr Skanda, the underdog. The intelligentsia always favours the underdog even if it has rabies. It's the British disease, you know. The way I see it, it's a three-cornered fight: between the JVP, the Tigers and the army. In reality, there are lots of revenge killings too, old scores being settled, but it's easier to blame one of the big three. Now rent-a-crowd, they just love to hate the army, so whatever happens the army gets the blame, because they're seen as the strongest of the three.'

'Are you sure? You sound unusually clear about this.'

She hiccupped gently. 'I must be drunk,' she said. 'I'm not usually this lucid.'

There was a crackle on the line. Mr Skanda was saying something she couldn't understand.

'What's that?'

But the line went dead. She could have sworn he had asked whether she needed a car.

From her position high up on the back balcony of her house three doors away, Mrs Rodrigo watched the doings at Serendipity with interest and concern. In her gold lurex headband and her electro-pink tights Mrs Rodrigo spent an inordinate amount of time on her fit-and-fold strider. She looked down sorrowfully at her thighs and they looked back in thunder. She had tried the no-carbs diet, she had tried the blood-group diet; she had tried the low-rent gym on Galle Road where a sweaty three-wheeler kariar called Viraj had tried, unsuccessfully, to train her (she shuddered at the recollection). She had even tried sex with Mr Rodrigo, for a very short while. Nothing had worked, alas. So it was back to her trusty fit-and-fold.

'Fit and fold, shit and hold,' she sang to herself as she strode along, 'fit and fold, shit and hold!' She wasn't normally of a scatological turn of mind, it was only the thought of her husband that made her so (the little shit).

This was the same Mrs Rodrigo who had so obligingly hidden Piyumi's mother, Mrs Segarajasingham, under her bed during the riots of 1983. A lot had changed since then. The bed for a start. No longer the homemade jackwood job by Moratuwa Lionel, the bed was now a square polished plinth of titanium cement on which a sprung mattress reposed. Even if Mrs Segar had wanted to hide under it now she couldn't.

The Rodrigos, too, had come a long way. In 1983, Mr Rodrigo had merely been a prosperous timber merchant, but the intervening years had been kind to him. Astute lobbying in the corridors of power had led to a total ban on imported tropical hardwood, leaving Mr Rodrigo in virtual sole charge of the local timber industry. And he went at it with the zeal of a young George Washington. No tree was spared the swish of his axe. At the same time, his propensity for good works bordered almost on the obscene.

Many bare hillsides and denuded forests later, he was one of Sri Lanka's richest, most beneficent men. You could sincerely say he had touched the entire country. (Certainly his axe had.) But then Mr Rodrigo hit a glass ceiling. He discovered that money isn't everything, particularly if you have rather too much of it. Politics was a welcome relief. He rose quickly through the ranks to where he now was, the minister for internal affairs. He also discovered that you cannot achieve anything in life without sacrifice, and of course the biggest sacrifice Mr Rodrigo made on his way up was his wife. After all, there is no point being in charge of internal affairs if you can't have an affair with an intern.

There was truly nothing Mr Rodrigo did not know about the internals of his interns.

There's usually a lot of press in a political career, and if you looked at the photos in chronological order you would see the Rodrigos increasing in size on an endless diet of wedding buffets as the months went by—in Sri Lanka everyone wants a minister as witness at his wedding —but always in the background if you looked closely there was an intern, fresh-faced and sari-clad, in a skimpy blouse offsetting a tantalizingly bare midriff. Then further along the line Mrs Rodrigo simply dropped out of the pictures.

She had discovered fit-and-fold.

She also discovered Rodrigo's Revenge; sometimes known as refurbishment. She opened the doors of her house to Colombo's most violent interior desecrator, with instructions that no expense was to be spared and no wall either. All was now marble and glass, brocade and brass.

Another aspect of Rodrigo's Revenge was foreign travel. Anyone knows that a country's internal affairs can only be solved by thorough and exhaustive research in the world's foreign capitals. Mrs Rodrigo travelled in a suite of her own—the interns in single rooms on the floor below, all in a row—and with every trip the house grew. After Disneyworld where the internal affairs' delegation went on a two-week fact-finding tour (they found the *Pirates of the Caribbean* particularly informative) Mrs Rodrigo installed the plastic trees in the plastic conservatory. After Venice, the Venetian windows. After Egypt she sprinkled the garden with obelisks. After Russia she put in the steps (because nobody bothered to tell her about the extra p in the spelling).

The minister signed cheque after cheque, lavishing gilt upon guilt. It was the least he could do. Indeed, Mrs Rodrigo looked upon her refurbishments as a sort of performance art. Architecturally they were the equivalent of her gym kit.

The back balcony on the third floor was the highest point in the neighbourhood, the three houses separating her from Serendipity being mere matchboxes. From there she watched the strange goings-on in the back pavilion.

Oh, look, there's that eccentric returnee girl again on the bottom rung of that ridiculous homemade ladder (two bamboos, lots of twine, say a prayer) and ooh, the shirtless suddha man on the top rung . . . he's losing his balance, ohmigod, he's about to fall! Get the paint you fool, get the paint, she's got the paint, the ladder's gone, he's on top of her ohmigod is he trying to kiss her? She's springing away now he's chasing after her, oh no, no, they've gone inside, damn, damn, damn . . .

Really it was better than Bollywood, better than any Sri Lankan teledrama. Binoculars, she said. I must get myself some binoculars.

10

None of the inhabitants of Serendipity went out to work (Work? What's work?) so it was something of a shock to the system when the doorbell rang at sharp eight in the morning. The doorbell itself was something of a shock to the system anyway, sounding as it did like a fire alarm or a summons to school dinner. Ten seconds later it rang again and by the time Suranganee had got to the gate whoever it was outside had his finger permanently on the bell .

Suranganee opened the gate. 'You think I'm on roller skates?' she asked.

'I have an appointment with Piyumi Segarajasingham,' said the self-important man outside. By then Suranganee had seen the car, pale green with large holes in the corroded bodywork. It had clattered up the drive to the front door.

'Wait here on the steps,' she ordered the stranger who made as if to climb up to the verandah. There were three points of reception in these old houses: the steps, the verandah, and if you were really special, one of the inner drawing rooms. Suranganee prided herself on recognizing quality when she saw it, or the lack of it in this case. (All except suddhas about whom she was, naturally, colour blind.)

'A cup of tea,' said the stranger loudly to her retreating back. 'Three sugars, no milk.'

Suranganee turned round.

'How about a Marie biscuit or two with that and a piece of chocolate cake? Try the Matara Tea Rooms down the bottom of the road.' Her laughter rang out sharply against the high ceilings of the house.

'Someone to see you,' she said waking Piyumi, who struggled downstairs in a semi-conscious state. She saw a silver-haired man with a silver beard, in white trousers and a white shirt. Closer inspection revealed a fraying collar, and trousers more grey than white.

'My name is L.M. Siddhu,' he said. He looked like an ageing Marxist, which indeed he was. His father had named him Lenin Marx Siddhu in an excess of enthusiasm (or perhaps it was to outdo the neighbour who had named his son Hitler Musso Wickremesinghe).

'Someone told me you needed a car.'

'That's interesting because someone told me the same thing.' She looked out at the car in the drive. She noticed a large hole near the petrol tank. One of the birds in the garden had alighted on it and was pecking away, attempting to make a nest inside.

'I've never driven here,' she said.

'You have a UK licence?'

'Yes, but I've never driven there either.'

'I have a driver for you.'

'That won't be necessary,' she said. 'I won't be needing your car.'

She thought of the aged Toyota Crown and how difficult it was to get Uncle Bala to drive her anywhere. He wouldn't let her borrow it either. In his canon women simply didn't drive.

'I don't have any money to hire it,' she said.

'You don't need money. It's yours for the duration of your stay.'

There's no such thing as a free lunch, a voice inside reminded her. Of course there is, you're in Sri Lanka, the land of free lunches, said another. She could smell danger. She could almost feel her tongue tingling with the taste of blood. But there was a wayward streak in her that relished the perverse: it was what had made her leave the safety of Knightsbridge for the razor-raw edge of Brixton.

'Leave it here,' she said all of a sudden.

He gave her the keys. 'The documents are in the car.' After he had gone, she realized she had no way of getting back in touch with him, no address or telephone number. Only a wildly improbable name.

The Heraths were very pleased with their new lodger. He hadn't complained about anything so far: the faulty geyser, the cracked loo seat, the polecats mating on the roof.

'A good Ceyesta mattress makes up for everything,' said Mrs Herath decisively.

It was amazing how tired he continued to look every morning after a good night's sleep.

One small thing worried them. Marek didn't seem to have made any friends. Apart from school, and that ditzy girl who had dropped him off that first day, he had no contact with the outside world. And nothing from abroad: no letters, no calls.

'Maybe he's gay,' suggested Mr Herath.

'Nonsense. He never smiles.'

They decided they had to do something to improve his social life.

As if on cue, a postcard from the UK arrived for him that morning. Mrs Herath took it into the privacy of her bedroom to read it, shutting the door behind her. It was one of those naughty postcards from the seaside. A rather plump Victorian bathing belle was bending over, exposing an expanse of frilly knicker. Love and kisses from Margate, it said.

'Dennis and I are here for a dirty weekend,' said the writing overleaf. 'And we don't wish you were here. Ma.'

'A mother like that, just imagine!' muttered Mrs Herath. 'Outrageous!'

More than ever they were resolved to help him. They tackled him as soon as he came home that evening.

'If you'd like to bring a friend over for Sunday lunch,' said Mr Herath, 'Dulcie will be making her beef smore and yellow rice.'

'Maybe there's a girl you'd like to invite?'

'Or even a boy?'

'Thanks,' said Marek noncommittally, leaving the Heraths to wonder, was that a no or a yes?

For weeks the watte had been buzzing with news of the minister's rally. Plastic buntings in party colours of gold and brown were strung from tenement to tenement. It didn't matter if you supported the minister or not. On that day you did. And a week later, when the opposition held their rally with streamers of orange and silver, you were definitely theirs for the day.

Elections were always a good time for those in the watte. The spirit of goodwill and generous bonhomie that pervaded the area managed to overcome, for that brief period, the miasma of open drains, rotting garbage and overflowing latrines that were the normal facts of their everyday life.

And then, and then! The highest point of it all: the free lunch packet. This was no longer the homemade job wrapped in newspaper or a banana leaf containing dried fish and giant grains of mildewed milchard. Nowadays it was fried rice and fried chicken and chilli paste, packaged in the finest non-biodegradable polystyrene that money could buy. (The minister was a great environmentalist.) On the front of the container, stamped in festive red were the letters Fuk-a-Luk Café, the very symbol of quality.

In order to earn this reward your job was very simple: you had to shout 'Jaya Wewa' at everything the minister said.

'Do not forget,' roared the minister, 'that in our term of office we have given you housing and electricity, hospitals and running water!'

'Jaya Wewa! Jaya Wewa!' roared the crowd joyfully. Viraj and Siddhu found themselves next to each other in the crowd. In between the Jaya Wewas they were able to conduct a normal everyday conversation.

'Can you drive a car? Jaya Wewa?' roared Siddhu.

'Jaya Wewa, of course, Jaya Wewa!' growled Viraj.

'Be on stand-by, Jaya Wewa. We may need you.'

'Jaya Wewa. Who pays the 250 on the three-wheeler? Jaya Wewa?'

'Don't ask silly questions, Jaya Wewa. You know we'll take care of it.'

The minister had got on to genetics, always a popular subject at these rallies.

'Never forget we're descended from the Aryans who came here from India 2500 years ago!' screamed the minister.

'Jaya Wewa!' roared the crowd.

Just recently a disturbing report had landed on the minister's desk about newly excavated settlements that pre-dated the Indian arrival by 500 years at least. The minister angrily slammed it into the Out tray. If these archaeologists didn't know the simple facts of history, they would bloody well have to go back to school and learn them!

The lunch boxes were distributed to an exhausted crowd, and it was only a matter of minutes before the salmonella in the chilli paste began to work its magic. People ran to the double row of latrines at the centre of the watte. There were already queues. Someone who couldn't wait had already decorated the floor of the adjacent bath-house. But by then the minister had departed with his entourage in a blaze of glory to a private lunch at the Hilton.

One of the special pleasures of a rally was that you got to see yourself on TV the same evening on the eight o'clock news, and Viraj got home to find everyone watching. There was a heavy bank of flowers around the mike. The minister was quite short, so at times it looked like the people were being harangued by a very lively bunch of carnations.

'Look, there's Siddhu!' said Viraj's grandma. They could see the silvery head bobbing up and down with surprising agility. He might have been at a disco. 'Bloody hypocrite!'

Viraj, who had been next to Siddhu, was blocked from view, alas, by fat Celestina from the next lane, who was jumping up and down ferociously, shouting Jaya Wewa! at the top of her voice. At times the camera shook.

'We have to talk about your wedding,' reminded Viraj's mum.

That was how it was done in Sri Lanka. You decided to have a wedding: then you went shopping for a bride.

Viraj threw up his hands. 'Time enough for that!'

'Now that you've got your three-wheeler and you're earning good money . . .' Viraj's three-wheeler was the envy of the watte.

'I have somebody,' he said, stunning everyone into silence. His grandma muted the TV. The shock was so great.

'You what?'

'I have somebody,' he repeated. 'A suddhi.'

This was really too much. There were very few pleasures afforded your average Sri Lankan family: political rallies at election time, wife-beating teledramas, and last but not least, family weddings and funerals. By choosing to marry a suddhi you were essentially depriving your family of all those simple pre-nuptial pleasures: the engagement, the selection of the bride's homecoming sari, those oddly formal visits to her relatives, the endless bitching about them afterwards. Only an insensitive and uncaring bridegroom would inflict such mental cruelty on his family.

'You'd better bring her round,' they warned. Viraj shrugged.

11

Driving Marek to Serendipity after school, Viraj noticed an odd cavalcade in the garden. There was a car—oh, my goodness, the car!—pale green and ancient with large holes in it. Inside was the love of his life, with that odd girl Marek came to see every day. Behind the car Suranganee was trying to salvage the remains of a stone bench the car had just demolished.

'Debs is taking me for a driving lesson,' Piyumi said happily to Marek. 'Do you want to come along?'

Viraj went round to Debs's side of the car. 'Machang!'

'Machang!'

He desperately wanted to be asked to stay, to join in the fun. It would have been plain good manners as far as he was concerned. But Debs was curiously unresponsive. Welcome to the wonderful world of Suddhaland, he thought.

He turned to Marek. 'Shall I wait for you?'

'I'll find my way back, thanks.'

With great reluctance he turned the three-wheeler out of the gates flashing red, blue, red, in what looked like a desperate show of bravado.

Every time Marek came in through these gates, he felt he was home. Kicking off his sandals he walked barefoot up the drive. For one whole week after his arrival he had carried his jacket over one arm like a sort of safety blanket. Then one daring morning he left it at home, and survived. A week later the long-sleeved shirts were replaced by short-sleeved ones. Out went the shoes next, in came sandals. He hadn't quite descended to the depths of Bata slippers in public though he wore them at home like a shameful secret, and of course at Serendipity. But he could see the day he succumbed looming large on the horizon.

He went round the side of the house to the back, switched the small radio on and began to stir yesterday's paint which had settled to the bottom of the pot.

After numerous false starts and a lot of jerking backwards and forwards like a recalcitrant baby elephant, the green car headed off out on the open road. Suranganee watched it with both hands on her head.

'Appo!' she said.

Piyumi's hand was closed firmly around the gear stick, Debs's closed firmly around hers. Serendipity stood on a wide tree-lined avenue with deep ditches on either side. A hundred yards up was the house of some minister, protected by a roadblock manned by a young cop.

He came out of the little tin hut that was his permanent place of residence. Inside it looked quite cosy with pictures of plump, green-eyed Hindi film stars and oiled musclemen.

'ID please.'

'No ID,' said Debs, mouthing the words slowly as if to a

child of four. 'Me foreign. Me Woman in Want,' she added, a little unnecessarily.

His mouth twitched. 'Me want too.' He turned to Piyumi.

'Oh, I'm not Sri Lankan,' said Piyumi, and felt like St. Peter denying Christ. 'I don't have an identity card.' The young cop looked at her passport. 'Tamil?'

Only half, she wanted to say, my mother is Sinhalese, but she bit the words back. She had betrayed her principles once already: that was enough.

'Tiger?'

The anger inside raged and boiled over. How dare you! she wanted to say. Not every Tamil is a Tiger. And nowadays, not every Tiger is a Tamil either. There are plenty of your countrymen selling their motherland downriver. But she thought in confusion: Your countrymen are my countrymen; so where does that leave the two of us?

Debs had pulled out a blue card. 'Look here. Me foreign NGO.'

'Ah,' he replied, 'then you White Tiger.'

And just as suddenly Piyumi's rage subsided, as if somebody had turned the gas off underneath. He's flirting with us, she thought with sudden clarity, it's his way of passing the time. He's bored shitless sitting inside that hut all day.

She noticed the thin gold cross around his neck. 'You're Catholic,' she said.

'Christian,' he corrected her proudly.

'So you're Tiger too. Isn't that what they say in this country, that all Christians are secret Tigers?'

The smile left his eyes. It was all right for him to joke with them. But not the other way round. He rolled back the barrier and signalled them through.

Sunday came and the Heraths waited with bated breath and beef smore for their luncheon party to arrive. They hadn't seen Marek all morning.

There was a tremendous clattering outside and an aged green Datsun drove up to the low gate on Deal Place. It was Marek. With that rather odd girl who had dropped him off that first day. Trying hard not to show their disappointment (the car, my goodness, the car!) they welcomed them in.

'Call me Dulcie,' said Mrs Herath, 'and he's Janaka.'

'What do you mean he?' countered Mr Herath. 'Please sit.'

The girl took a quick look at the divan, pulled a cushion off it and settled herself on the floor, tucking her feet up under her like a cat.

Mrs Herath could see this was going to be difficult. Not that she minded her good Barbara Sansoni cushions on the floor—God knows her floor was clean enough, she had only mopped it that morning—it was the sheer domestic aggression of the act, the violence to her carefully planned interior.

'What would you like to drink, dear?'

'Iced water for me,' said Marek.

'I'd love a glass of beer,' said Piyumi. Beer was the one thing they didn't have.

'I could do you a good shot of arrack,' said Mr Herath, 'gal or pol?'

'Janaka,' said Mrs Herath, quelling him in an instant. The girl finally settled for Passiona and they all sat there looking at each other goodnaturedly. This went on for quite a while.

Finally Mrs Herath said, 'The elections.'

'Yes, the elections,' said Marek.

'My brother-in-law is contesting, you know.' Nobody seemed interested in the brother-in-law so she dropped the subject. Then she looked down and noticed with horror the Bata slippers on Marek's feet. Now there was no reason why he shouldn't have been in Bata slippers in his own home—this was his own home, Mrs Herath had made that very clear the first day—but to wear slippers to a lunch party! And a suddha too! The shame of it drove her headlong into the kitchen where she summoned Mr Herath.

'Slice the meat,' she barked, she was so annoyed.

At the table Marek said: 'I'll eat with my fingers.' The girl followed suit, leaving the Heraths brandishing their implements shamefacedly. It was like bearing arms against the innocent.

Years ago, when the Heraths had first returned, they'd had a lodger. Mr Souza from Kotahena was caramel-coloured. He'd sported a great line in cravats, wore socks with sandals, and on particularly hot days wore a handkerchief on his head knotted at the four corners: all those great British customs the Heraths had never actually seen any Englishman practise. He spoke frequently of home, home being London not Kotahena, though it soon became apparent he had never been there. He listened to Elgar in the evenings.

The Heraths were thrilled with their good fortune which continued till one day, coming home early from work,

Mr Souza discovered Mr Herath in a loud checked sarong and hil-hil vest from the Mouse of Passion. Things were never quite the same again and a month later Mr Souza gave notice and left.

They'd had such high hopes for Marek! They watched him gloomily, slurping down great handfuls of rice and curry while little brown rivulets of sauce trickled down from his fingers to his wrist. Mrs Herath hastily retired to the kitchen to prepare two finger bowls. Mr Herath cleared the dishes and brought in the pudding.

'Dulcie's famous chocolate mousse,' he announced.

Marek held up his right hand. 'Aren't I a mess?' He looked round for the finger bowls which hadn't yet arrived. 'Oh never mind, I still have another,' he said and plunged his left hand into the chocolate mousse. 'So much tastier when you use your fingers, don't you think?'

When the guests had left the Heraths looked at each other in consternation. It was one thing for your Englishman to go native; another for it to happen before your very eyes. How they longed for the pomp and circumstance of Souza!

'We have to rescue him,' said Mrs Herath. 'For the sake of olde England.' Actually she didn't say that last bit but she meant it. 'Of all the decent Colombo Seven girls he could have chosen . . .'

Then suddenly, simultaneously, the same thought occurred to both, the blue spark of electricity crackling from one pair of eyes to the other.

'Poopie!' they shouted at each other joyously.

Marek and Piyumi drove round and round the leafy lanes and crescents of Colombo Seven. It was their favourite occupation now they had the car. Sunday afternoon was particularly satisfying: everybody was fast asleep after their rice and curry.

'I think,' said Marek moodily, 'I think I'm ready to try that sarong now.'

12

There were actually so many elections in Sri Lanka—provincial, general, presidential—that the inhabitants of its capital had long since ceased to care what they were for. They were happy just to go along for the ride. A regular election was, quite simply, the biggest thing on the city's social calendar, like the carnival in Rio or the Mardi Gras in New Orleans. And like those two, there were rallies, there were parades, there were performers.

Among the candidates this year there were beauty queens and cutie queens and plain old queens. There were master pastors and past masters. There were priests and there were sinners. Crack teams of poster pasters were deployed in the early hours of every morning to deface the city walls. Other crack teams were deployed just half an hour later to deface the posters of the first lot. One candidate had had his eyes removed with almost surgical precision from the posters about an hour after they went up. Everybody agreed his face looked tremendously improved.

To ferry these fly-by-night teams around there were anonymous white vans, sometimes with no visible number plates. They were useful for kidnapping rival politicians or the twelve-year-old sons of rich men. (Nobody kidnapped the wives, there was a very real danger they wouldn't be wanted back.) What everybody needed was money. The rich stole from the poor, the poor stole the manhole covers off the drains. There were various explosions and small fires all over the city. These were variously blamed on the JVP, the Tigers and the government. Sometimes they were blamed on faulty electrical wiring. It was murder out there and the denizens of Colombo wisely kept to their homes, promising their votes to everyone and anyone who asked politely.

Piyumi came home to find a family conclave going on.

'They've been waiting for you,' said Suranganee with barely disguised satisfaction. Suranganee hadn't been happy with the goings-on in the servants' quarters. She had a very strong sense of what was right and what was wrong. It was plainly wrong for Lenin Marx Siddhu to demand a cup of tea of her. (Who did he think he was, the little tenement dweller? And she, the sole help of a grand Colombo Seven house!) It was even more wrong for a suddha to be painting the servants' quarters. And shirtless too. Next thing you knew they'd be wanting to move in, the brazen duo!

Piyumi opened the door to the TV room and they all looked up.

'You can stop all this painting nonsense immediately. You won't be moving in any time soon.'

'Who says?'

'We've taken legal advice. You were left a seventh of the undivided share of Serendipity.'

'But the subdivision has already been approved.'

'Not by the court, it hasn't.'

'But you agreed!'

'We've changed our minds. If you persist, we'll take you to court. We'll say that the fair and equitable solution is to sell the property in one piece. It's six of us against you. You don't stand a chance.'

Piyumi could see her American cousin flexing and unflexing his bicep, clenching and unclenching his fist. He didn't look at her, but the action said it all. She got up from the table in a rage.

'You can't stop me occupying any part of the house I want. You know it was always understood . . .'

'That green contraption of yours,' Bala interrupted. 'Kindly park it at the back in future. It lowers the tone.'

'What does Sinnetambe say to all this?' she demanded.

They looked at her in silence.

'I'll ask him myself then.' She turned back to them at the door.

'By the way,' she said sweetly, 'you can all fuck off, the lot of you.'

She drove the car off at great speed, rattling and rolling, up to the roadblock.

'Passport?'

She was in no mood for flirtatious cops. 'It's at home,' she snapped. It was, in fact, in the glove compartment but she wanted to test her strength.

'I might have to search you,' he said looking down her cleavage. She glared at him.

He rolled back the barrier and let her through.

'Mr Sinnetambe is in a meeting,' his secretary said, 'I'll just see when he'll be free.' By then Piyumi had already walked through the room and opened the inter-connecting door.

Mr Sinnetambe was alone at an empty desk. He was cleaning the dirt under his nails with a letter-opener and periodically admiring the results.

'What's this about a court case?' she roared.

He looked up startled. 'Miss Segarajasingham, please sit down and calm yourself. I have advised them on the legal position. If they take you to court there's every chance you'll lose.' He looked at her across the desk. 'I have been a family friend for over fifty years. I have acted for your great-grandfather and all his children. Believe me, I have your best interests at heart.'

'And I suppose you were the one who advised my mother to sell everything and emigrate,' she said bitterly.

'Are you telling me your mother isn't happy?'

'Who said anything about happiness?' she asked sadly.

As she came out of Sinnetambe's office she felt her legs buckle slightly under her, and she had to sit down in the waiting room.

'Are you all right?' the secretary asked. She nodded.

'I just need a few moments.'

Looking round the room with its impersonal furnishings, its bright abstract paintings on the walls, she suddenly realized what they meant by the treachery of the tropics: where the cruelty was as much a highlight as the beauty; where plants, animals, people were all as deadly as they were beautiful. In temperate climates they worked to a much more restricted palate, restricted in terms of colour and emotion and danger; an altogether more mature existence yet strangely more innocent. No wonder these Westerners can't handle the violence of our deaths, she thought, the gratuitous expressionism of our cruelty. Here I am in paradise and there are snakes all around me and I am alone. But almost simultaneously with this thought she found herself coming over all Hindu: I am here because I am meant to be: it is written.

Instinctively, she squared her shoulders.

'Shall I see if Mr Sinnetambe is free to see you now?'the secretary asked.

Piyumi got up. 'I've seen as much of him as I need to,' she said. 'I'm afraid there's nothing more he can do for me now.'

Downstairs she knocked on the door of Women in Want. But Debs was away at a meeting.

'She won't be back in the office till tomorrow,' they said.

'Bloody woman,' thought Piyumi angrily. 'All over you when you don't want her. Never there when you do.'

13

Down at the gym they had cut the electricity for non-payment of bills. This state of affairs was well into its second week now, so the excuse given by management—repairs to the main power-line from the road—was beginning to wear a bit thin. In the evening they lit candles. The members wandered about groping in the dark, dropping weights. Every once in a while you heard the crack of someone's big toe.

This was where Debs's meeting was; where she could be found every afternoon after three. Whether her staff knew this wasn't clear. But she possessed, courtesy of the office, that wonderful new invention, the mobile phone. It was the cynosure of all eyes at the gym as she carried it from machine to machine, placing it reverently on the floor while she did her reps. Members of the gym coveted the mobile almost more than they coveted her.

Viraj was helping her with chin-ups. He had a hand firmly under each buttock as she heaved herself up to the bar and down, grunting. She was the only woman he knew with arms and shoulders powerful enough for chin-ups. For that matter, there were hardly any men who could do them either.

'Have dinner with me,' he said, the words escaping his mouth unexpectedly. 'Machang,' he added, so she would know his intentions were entirely honourable. Then he stopped in confusion. The last thing he wanted was an honourable intention. He was looking for a date plus plus.

She came down to the floor with a groan. Lovely guy! she thought. A bloke's night out was what she really needed. Men gave you uncomplicated love, affection, admiration: they were like dogs, really. Women now, they were a different species altogether. Tricky, dark creatures with hidden agendas and gothic subtexts. Women were good for one thing only. (She thought of the notches on her bedpost.)

'Great!' she said. 'Machang.'

After gym they walked along the Galle Road to Sirisanda where Viraj's friends hung out. How his stock would go up when they saw him with this white beauty! Disappointingly, he could see no one he knew.

Between them they put away copious quantities of roti and mutton curry, Debs rolling up her sleeves and getting down to it with gusto. In the far corner a door opened, throwing a pale blue neon light into the restaurant. Inside, Viraj could see a woman seated on a bed, coiling up her hair, taking pins out of her mouth and sticking them in. She caught him looking at her and smiled tiredly.

Two men came out. She must have given them a special deal, he thought, two for the price of one. They came and hovered over him and he realized with a shock they were from the watte.

'They say you're in with that little turd, Siddhu. Better watch your step, fucker.'

They were gone before he could think of a suitable reply.

'What did they say?' Debs asked.

'They were admiring your beautiful blonde hair.'

Afterwards they walked along Galle Road, neon-lit under a starry sky. He took her hand.

What a lovely guy! she thought again. She was indeed blessed to have friends like this, friends who enabled her to see this country from inside out. So many of her foreign colleagues knew only the five-star hotels, the swimming club, the embassy cocktail circuit.

What a compliment that he has taken my hand. That's what men do all over the East when they're especially affectionate towards each other. They walk hand in hand!

Students of the Mogambo International were expected to be in school by sharp at ten minutes to eight in the morning for registration, with classes starting at eight thirty. In practice, old hands like Iresha and Princy strolled in any time before nine.

The teachers reported in by seven thirty. That morning when Marek arrived, all was chaos and confusion.

'The Chairman of the Board of Governors,' said Percy ffinch-Percy tersely. 'Surprise visit.'

Mrs Leelaratne had been given the task of arranging the flowers. Ikebana was not her strong suit but she was gamely making a go of it with crab claws harvested from the garden and ornamental bamboo.

ffinch-Percy himself was breaking cobwebs with a broom tied to a long bamboo pole, looking as if he'd just flown in fresh from a game of Quidditch. He wore a pink frilly apron that matched the high colour of his cheeks but clashed horribly with his carrot hair.

Opening the door to the computer room he vigorously evicted its occupant.

'The gates, Fernando, the gates! How many times do I have to tell you you're not on the computers today, you're on the gates.'

Fernando came out unwillingly. He had only recently been promoted from security guard to ICT. To go back, even for a day, was difficult. But there'd be trouble if there was nobody to open the gate for the Governor. Fernando was Marek's closest friend at school. The children called him I-Hear-the-Drums Fernando. A skinny young man with finely drawn features and an unusual propensity for making people fall in love with him, Fernando left two children under three and a harassed wife at home every morning to escape to school, where he spent the whole day at the gate, cadging loans off anyone foolish enough to succumb to his charm and hard luck stories.

Recently promoted to ICT where the prestige was greater but the pickings fewer, he now had a host of daily young mothers anxious to check on their children's progress. His class had swelled considerably. Unfortunately, nobody nowadays lent him money. They fell in love with him instead, to the intense annoyance of his wife.

Marek and he found they were very similar. Both suffered

from love: one from a surfeit, the other from a lack. Fernando knew all about unrequited love too; from the other end, so to speak. 'People call me all hours,' he complained. 'They won't get off the phone. The other day the wife unplugged it and threw it in the bin. It took me hours to clean the baby vomit off it.'

By nine, the premises were as ready as they would ever be. Even Iresha and Princy had turned up. 'Do you like Percy's pinny?' he whispered. 'Christmas present from me.'

In the event, the Governor's chauffeur-driven Mercedes rolled in at eleven, exactly two hours late. He was followed by a personal assistant who carried his briefcase and his mobile, which rang incessantly.

The Governor talked into it incessantly.

He paused once to look at ffinch-Percy sternly. 'Are you in drag?'

Percy looked down at the apron he had forgotten to take off, and tittered. 'Well, yes, I suppose I am, really.'

The Governor looked at Marek. 'You're the new boy,' he said. 'Barely out of nappies, aren't you?'

He took Percy into his office and shut the door, leaving the PA on guard outside.

'Numbers are down,' he said. 'What are you going to do about it?'

'A publicity drive, perhaps? A fête? A fashion show?'

'They're denouncing international schools again. Always a popular measure at election time. They're an insult to our free education system, they say. They instil all the wrong Western values.'

'But most ministers send their children to international schools! They're more Westernized than anyone else.'

'Of course. It's what we in the trade call slash-and-burn technology. Get your own family across first. Burn everything behind so nobody else can follow.' The Governor was lost in thought for a moment. Then he looked up.

'Numbers. I want a proposal on my desk by the end of the week.'

A lack of official patronage meant these schools were run like business ventures. Anything to keep the numbers up. Extra books in the library didn't get you your numbers, nor extra equipment in the lab. All-singing all-dancing stage spectaculars did; preferably with all-white leads. So that prospective parents could congratulate each other saying, really, it had turned out all white on the night.

'A fashion show,' mused Percy ffinch-Percy. 'Now I wonder . . .'

Marek came out of class that evening to find the green car waiting for him.

'I thought I'd come and see your place of work,' she said. Time was hanging heavy on Piyumi's hands. Nothing seemed to be working out. At the same time, there was intense pressure on her to decide quickly.

Her mother had called in the morning. 'What's this nonsense I hear about you wanting to keep the servants' quarters?'

'Well, it's not as if we need the money,' she replied defensively.

'Piyumi. Darling. Listen to me.' She could hear her mother take a deep breath. 'How do you think I managed to put you through public school? Through university? Who do you think's going to look after me in my old age? I can see it's not going to be you.'

Piyumi let her rant and rave like this for a while. She held the phone away from her to show non-compliance, to show how far she was above all this talk of rupees and cents. It was a pity nobody could see. Still, it made her feel good.

'Piyumi? Piyumi! Are you there?'

'Yes, Ma,' she said wearily. 'I'll let you know once I've decided.'

'They've been calling you from work,' her mother said, a parting shot aimed with deadly accuracy. 'I don't know how long I can stave them off for. You'd better get back quick or you may not have a job to come back to.'

Piyumi looked at the receiver gone dead in her hands.

'That's if I want to come back,' she said to no one in particular.

She told Marek the bad news as soon as he got into the car.

'They're all determined to sell Serendipity, so I may not be allowed to keep my bit. I'm probably wasting everyone's time and money trying to fight this thing. The really bad part,' she continued sadly, 'is that we were never really close to any of these relations. I now seem to be destroying what little goodwill there ever was between us.'

He thought of his own mother and her passion for selling everything she could lay her hands on.

'Look, it's not some romantic dream is it, this little piece of Serendipity? Can you really see yourself at some point of your life coming back to live here?'

'Yes,' she said fiercely. 'Yes, yes! To both those questions.'

His heart leapt when she said this: more than anything he wanted her to stay, to move in, to finish the painting; he couldn't bear to think of her going back.

'You need to act as if it's all going to happen the way you want it. These things have a sort of self-fulfilling way about them.' But he knew as he said this, that there was a large dose of selfishness motivating his words.

They drove for a bit in silence.

'By the way,' she said. 'Who's that hottie you were talking to at the gate?'

'Hottie?' He had to think a bit. 'Oh, that's Fernando from ICT.'

'Phew!' She fanned her face with her hand to show how hot.

'What's he got that I haven't?' he thought gloomily.

14

Elections were only a fortnight away. All over the city you could see cardboard cut-outs of the minister. The artist had painted him rather fatter than he actually was, and an improbable shade of salmon pink: this was what the people wanted, no demanded. A thin and dark leader could never command the respect of the country. Sales of skin whitening creams such as Boiled and Beautiful soared during election time.

Mrs Rodrigo looked down at her trim tummy, her firm thighs. Elections were the one time of year her husband actually needed her: to cut the ribbon at countless beauty salons, to cuddle countless babies, to sit next to him at countless film premières looking fat and fair. Fat and fair? Well, they were all in for a big surprise. The more she exercised the slimmer she got, the darker she became. This year she was going to be the Dark Lady of the Elections.

She looked around her as she strode up and down the balcony. Things were quiet at Serendipity this morning. They were probably all asleep, the lazy lot. Then she heard an altercation near her own gates and spotted an old lady berating the ministerial security.

Dulcie! She hurried down to deal with it.

Mrs Herath had no problem with the young cop at the roadblock. She jabbed at him with her umbrella, terrorized him with a few choice English phrases and in no time at all she was through. The guards at the ministerial gate were more problematic.

'My sister,' she said jabbing at the acid yellow palazzo looming beyond the obelisks, 'in there!'

The guards looked sceptically at her no-nonsense iron grey bun, her M&S crimplene slacks (fifteen years and still going strong), her Thatcheresque polyester blouse with the oversize bow. A relation of the minister's wife? Impossible!

But there was the minister's wife, shouting at them from the door to let her in.

'Evangeline!'

'Dulcie!'

'My, but you've pulled down!'

'I have, haven't I?' said Mrs Rodrigo proudly. Mrs Herath was looking around the room.

'That's new,' she said, pointing to a stuffed polar bear. 'From our last Alaskan cruise. Ranjith was investigating the possibilities of a salmon smokery in Colombo. You know, smoked salmon for the masses. Omega-3 for all.'

The polar bear was fat and fair. It would have made a very good election candidate.

'I could murder a cup of coffee,' said Mrs Herath hopefully.

'No caffeine after nine in the morning.'

'A piece of cake then? I'm starving.'

'Absolutely not!'

'Never mind, I'll wait for lunch.'

'I've banned lunch,' said Mrs Rodrigo firmly, 'till elections are over.'

'Well at least you can ask me to sit down.'

They sat down and put their heads together, and Mrs Herath began outlining the plan she was about to cook up: it was, alas, the only thing cooked up in the ministerial residence that day.

From deep within her dream Piyumi heard the sounds of an altercation floating somewhere above her bed. Cautiously, she tried opening an eye. She thought she could see Ganga above her, holding one end of a measuring tape. The other end was in the hands of a woman in plaits with jingling-jangling earrings. They seemed to be measuring her recumbent form.

'I'm not dead yet,' she wanted to shout out, but of course she couldn't. It's only a bad dream, she told herself.

Piyumi occupied the smallest room in the house—it had been a dressing room in its day—its only perceived advantage now being that it was next to the wet-and-wild bathroom. Its fifteen-foot-high ceilings made you feel you were inside a coffin standing on end. As in any coffin the acoustics were terrible, and the noise of the quarrel reverberated around her.

'Don't mind her,' Ganga was saying, 'she'll be gone in no time.'

'No!' Piyumi wanted to shout. 'No! No!' The dream was turning into a nightmare.

'In that case this room will do nicely for my son!' the woman in plaits exclaimed.

Ganga said something about her dead body.

'PhD from Oxford Street College,' continued the woman. 'ACBT, CIMA.' Their voices faded as they left the room.

'Welsh . . .'

Piyumi tried pulling the sheet over her head but sleep was now impossible. She dragged herself out of bed. Suranganee no longer brought up her early morning coffee so she padded down to the back kitchen, deep in the bowels of the house, where the cook was sitting on the floor listlessly peeling onions.

She had to bludgeon her with words to get the wood fire going and put the kettle on. She would have bludgeoned her with the kettle if it had taken any longer. (There was a perfectly good gas cooker in the front kitchen which the cook never used because she didn't trust these newfangled notions; Piyumi would have made the coffee there herself but the cook was in possession of the kettle.)

The coffee tasted odd, bitter.

'I've poisoned it,' said the cook grinning gummily.

'That's not funny,' said Piyumi. She nursed the mug carefully as she went back up to her bedroom.

It occurred to her that there was a slow war of attrition going on here: all the inhabitants of Serendipity were ranged against her. Conversations stopped when she entered the room. The washing machine was always unaccountably busy when she needed it; her clothes always the last to be taken off the line when it rained.

I have to mend my fences, I have to make it up to these people, she thought. If I somehow get to stay—and I will! Think positive, I will!—they are all I have.

At lunch Ganga announced, 'I'm fed up with all these brokers. I'm going to advertise in the *Sunday Observer*.'

'Good!' said Bala. 'It's never too late to find a partner.'

'The only thing about advertising is, we'll get all sorts of riff-raff traipsing through the house.'

'At your age you can't afford to be choosy.' Pushpam quelled him with a look.

A never-ending stream of brokers could be found at all hours, poking about in unwanted corners. They were all universal in their condemnation of the house.

Look at the roof, the horror of it! The walls are cabook, they won't last, of course. And oh, my goodness, the guttering!

Piyumi wanted to reply: every inch of the roof is Burma teak, and Burma teak is virtually indestructible. That's why they used it those days. The cabook's lasted a hundred years. What makes you think it won't last a hundred more? As for the guttering, it's good Victorian cast iron. A darned sight better than today's PVC which will twist and warp in no time.

But she held her peace. There was no point causing any more ill-will. Any argument was counterproductive until or unless she had a plan of her own: and she didn't.

'I have to get away for a few days,' she told Marek. 'It's

killing me having to listen to all these people bad-mouth Serendipity.'

'There's this place Fernando's always talking about. Down south. You think the car can make it?'

Marek got the number from Fernando, and they called. 'Two singles please, full board.'

'Is that local or foreign?' The receptionist at the other end prided himself on recognizing an English accent at a hundred paces. Foreign rates were at least twice as much.

'Local,' said Piyumi firmly. 'One under the name of Ms Segarajasingham, and the other for . . .' she caught herself in time, 'for Mr Segarajasingham.'

You could almost hear the receptionist's eyebrows go up.

'Singles are virtually the same price as doubles. You'd be much better off in one double.'

'We like our sleep,' said Piyumi quickly. 'You see, he snores.'

Early, on Sunday morning the phone began to ring, and simultaneously, the doorbell. How people could have figured out the address from a newspaper ad which omitted to mention it was anyone's guess, but figure it out they did. Friends, neighbours, well-wishers: all came to have a good snoop. Nobody had the slightest intention of buying. The brokers were outraged. By throwing Serendipity on the open market, Ganga was depriving them of their three per cent commission. They immediately played their ace of spades—the Nigerian from Magazine Road.

'If you just give me your personal bank account details,' he said, 'I'll see to it the money's transferred straightaway. There's millions lying unclaimed.'

Then there were the hoteliers and restaurateurs.

'This is perfect for an exclooziv restaurant,' said one. 'We can have Russian girls performing cabaret downstairs.'

'Is that what they call it nowadays?' asked Ganga acidly.

'And just one or two rooms upstairs for those too drunk to drive home, of course.'

'Of course.'

Finally, there were the architects and heritage people. 'This sort of bastard Palladianism,' said one, 'is an insult to our heritage. It only exposes our servile colonial mentality.'

'Nothing like a tasty piece of Corbusier,' said another wistfully. 'Asia's first modern woman architect came from Sri Lanka. I simply don't understand why we can't go on from there. Are we so short of modern women?'

'Bawa,' said a third, 'Bawa, Bawa, Bawa!' He sounded a little like a dog barking.

By the end of the day there were two firm offers. One for a boutique Chinese karaoke (an exclooziv concept in entertainment); the other from a developer who would knock down the whole bag of tricks and put up a steel and glass palace. They could all buy themselves flats at discount.

Ganga went to bed filled with a certain sense of satisfaction. Nobody thought to tell Piyumi. She was far away down south with Marek.

The road to Bentota, possibly like the road to hell, was paved with election rallies. As beach after beach unrolled to their right, Piyumi realized afresh how easy it was to fall in love with this country. Everywhere there were vast cut-outs of candidates, fringed with brown and gold or orange and silver depending on the party. At Panadura, they inadvertently joined a cycle race but the cyclists sped on, their skinny spandex bottoms bobbing up and down like trumpet stops, leaving the car sputtering in their wake. At Kalutara they passed a tall blonde woman addressing the crowd. 'My name is Ulla,' she said in flawless Sinhala. On they went. At Bentota all was calm. Till they tried to check in.

The clerk at reception greeted them with a big smile. 'Ah, the wedding party. We've reserved the honeymoon suite.'

'There's been some mistake. We specifically reserved two singles. We must have separate rooms.'

'That bad already, huh? Sorry, no can do. The party convention's on and all the candidates are here. We're chock-a-block as it is. It's the last big meet before elections.'

Yes! thought Marek. Yes! Yes! He tried not to let it show on his face. They could see the election candidates by the pool with their beer and bites, swishing about in enormous bermudas, gold medallions glinting on furry chests. There was loud music by the Cripsies and a few were attempting to baila with each other like dogs half-heartedly attempting to mate.

'I hope they govern better than they dance,' whispered Piyumi.

'We've sent up a complimentary love cake,' said the clerk

hopefully. 'Also a bottle of milk wine. Enjoy. And don't worry,' he added as an afterthought, 'it does get better. You have to work at it, though. Thirty years, my mother says. That's why I never married.'

There was a large double bed in the room. Also a bath big enough for two.

'You stick to your side of the bed,' warned Piyumi darkly, 'I'll stick to mine.'

'Understood,' said Marek. A little too promptly.

In the event his hand did stray, and before they knew it they were entwined. She was anyway far too good a person to say no to anyone who asked nicely.

'Oh, all right,' she said with a sort of fond familiarity. Then she shut her eyes and thought of Serendipity.

Afterwards they talked long into the night in the tradition of lovers. She told him how much the country was beginning to get to her, how important it was for her to save even that smallest piece of Serendipity. It pained him that her plans didn't seem to include his presence in any way, or his well-being. But he was used to sadness: at times it seemed to him his whole life was one long sadness, so this was nothing new, nothing unexpected. If I wait it out long enough she might change her mind, he thought with the sort of futile optimism that was hard-wired into his regret. So he put his own troubles aside and concentrated on hers. There is room for only one set of sorrows in any relationship.

'Maybe you could buy Serendipity,' he suggested.

'Yeah, right.'

'No, I mean it. If you could get your mother to sell one of her flats. In fact I could help, I have money in the bank.'

'No,' she said immediately. It was too easy, too pat. She didn't want to be under obligation to anybody, least of all Marek. Too much was expected of her in that quarter. There was only one way she could repay such a loan and it was too big a sacrifice as far as she was concerned.

Next morning there was a rose on their table. The manager came up with a worried look on his face.

'I have bad news,' he said. 'I know you lovebirds are just dying to get into the pool. But I'm afraid you can't. We've had to shut it down.'

'Oh?'

'It's the dear deputy minister for solid waste, lovely man! He's so used to passing resolutions and amendments. Well, it seems last night he passed something else.' The manager wrung his hands helplessly. 'I don't know why he didn't use the sea. Everyone else does. We'll have to drain the pool and sterilize it. It's caused a much bigger stink than that last IMF loan.'

They drove back late on Sunday night.

'Will you take over?' she asked halfway through. 'I'm tired.' There was a necklace of lights strung out over the horizon from fishing boats far away at sea. She purred gently in her sleep by his side as he negotiated the car over the railway tracks at Payagala and into the dreary endless suburbs of Colombo, their myriad neon-lit shops each selling the identical T-shirt, the exact same tin of canned fish, the ubiquitous packet of powdered milk.

It was as if they'd been married years and years and were returning from their usual weekend on the coast. I wouldn't want anything more than this, he thought. I wouldn't want her to love me, this is enough. Dear God, he prayed, is this really too much to ask?

You couldn't really call Marek a religious type, though with Polish parents you might have expected it. Indeed, his mother was. Her religion was the religion of incense and candle wax, medals and holy water. But she also believed in tarot cards and tea leaves and the lines on the palm of your hand. She read every horoscope she could lay her hands on, including ones from six-month-old newspapers picked up off the pavement.

'It says here last July I had money problems. I also met a tall dark stranger. That must have been Dr Khan when I went to him about my vertigo.'

'Ma, Dr Khan is five foot nothing. And last July you had just sold the ground floor. You were rich!'

'Well, they can't get everything right, can they?' Every Sunday they attended St. Mary's Clapham, a Victorian Gothic church with a Polish priest, Father Stanislaus, who believed in quantity rather than quality with services lasting an hour and a half sometimes. Marek, who was used to forty-five minutes maximum, in and out, would try to time it to arrive just after the sermon and leave just after communion. He sometimes got this badly wrong, arriving after everything had finished, because Father Stan had suddenly surprised them all with a lightning half-hour service. It was a game of wits, like Paper, Scissors, Stone. On those days Father Stan greeted him with a victorious smile as Marek made his mistimed entrance into a swiftly emptying church.

Marek's father never attended Mass, considering this women's business. But he came to the après-mass religiously, mingling with fellow Poles to discuss the horses. This took place in the forecourt of St. Mary's where the society of St. Vincent de Paul, the Little Sisters of the Poor and various other religious rattled their alms boxes hungrily at you. Marek's mother gave to them all, buying holy pictures and little plaster statuettes with gilded haloes.

'It's all money in the bank,' she would say. This was her investment in the afterlife, the stocks and bonds that paid dividends beyond the grave.

At one corner of the forecourt was a monumental mason, with funeral sculpture in the window. She pointed to a white marble angel on a rock reading a prayer book. 'That's the one I want.' For her the afterlife would begin on a baroque note, with trumpets and French horns and a Chandos Anthem or two.

Marek found all this carrying-on quite interesting, in the way a doctor finds his ward patients interesting: you could see that the antibiotics were necessary even though you didn't take them yourself.

His own religion was of that spare, astringent kind: the single spark blazing forth from the mind to the wide open universe beyond, as someone once said. Death was only your union with God, and life only a continuous submission to His will. He would have preferred his religion within the soaring celestial spaces, the reed-thin columns of true Gothic, not the crowded domesticity of the sham Victorian one. But he quite understood if God Himself had no architectural preferences.

This God was in any case something of an embarrassment to him. He seemed to be the God of the elderly, the cranky Polish pensioners with war medals, the twittering old ladies in black veils. He wasn't the God of tattooed blokes who worked on building sites. Marek preferred to keep his God a secret, a medal worn close to his heart.

The other thing that worried him hugely was serendipity, the occurrence of those happy accidents of chance. Who took the credit for those? Were they part of some divine obstacle course put there to test your reactions? Or were you free to blunder through, as with pretty much all else in life?

15

The men in the white van had been watching Lenin Marx Siddhu for days. An old hand from the JVP insurrection days of 1971, he had a sixth sense about these things: he knew he was being watched. Actually, there was nothing he could do about it. They knew where he lived in the watte, they knew his connection to Viraj. What he had to conceal was the line of communication to his handlers.

He had been warned when first recruited: 'You'll have all the financial backing you need but if you're caught, that's it, you're on your own.' Frequently he wondered whether it was worth it. But the rewards were dizzyingly spectacular: the freshly minted fake UK visa in his Sri Lankan passport. He knew all too well what this would lead to: a lifetime in front of the deep-fat fryer at McDonald's; or a member of a crack team of lavatory cleaners at Heathrow Airport. He was too old a hand to have any illusions about this. But anything was preferable to ending your days in the watte.

The watte was conveniently situated at one end of Colombo Seven, between the golf course and the cemetery. As far as wattes went, it was one of the posher ones. Everyone knew that it was only a matter of time before the minister dished out deeds to legitimize the squatters' claims. He had promised as much at that last rally.

Lenin Marx Siddhu's house was at one end of the watte, in a cul-de-sac. It was unusually quiet that full moon Poya evening; no one was around. He was walking home with a siri-siri bag of provisions when he noticed the van. It was white with black contact film pasted on the windows. He noticed its lack of a number plate. It was a narrow lane, and he squeezed past and continued walking. The important thing was not to let them know you knew. His legs tingled. It took him back to his childhood, to school races as he crouched under the starting gun.

The van suddenly turned its lights full on. As if he had heard the shot he uncoiled himself and began to sprint. He could hear the van pick up speed behind him. There was no room to get to a side. He could almost feel the smoky breath of its exhaust fumes on his neck as it closed in on him. In a last desperate act he turned and hurled his bag at the windscreen and in that split second, reached the high cemetery wall. He scrabbled over, dropping to the ground on the inside, panting. But there was no time to stop.

He picked himself up and ran. He had practised this escape route many times but he was not as young as he used to be. Never mind, he thought, if I have a heart attack at least I have come to the right place. He ran between angels with broken marble wings and forbidding black granite obelisks, finally reaching the small Palladian chapel of rest.

And there he rested.

The men in the white van braked suddenly, cursing. One of them put his hand out to pick bits of squashed tomato and rice off the windscreen. There was no danger of them following L.M. Siddhu into the graveyard. He was sure to come to a far stickier end at the hands of the ghosts in there. On full moon nights the graves opened and they walked about freely, everyone knew that. Good luck to him! They reversed the van back up the cul-de-sac.

The reason why this end of the watte was so deserted tonight was because there was a small function going on elsewhere, and everyone had gone to watch. Like those patient onlookers at a film première in Leicester Square they awaited the arrival of the stars with a delicious frisson of excitement. In the meantime they discussed the décor, the chain of fairy lights strung from the banana tree in the front yard of the house to the television aerial on the asbestos roof. It flashed red and blue alternately. There were those who thought the colour scheme too austere. They compared it unfavourably to the Christmas décor at that marvellous store on Duplication Road, the Mouse of Passion. There the lights flashed purple and green and orange, a far more satisfying combination.

Their musings were interrupted by the arrival of the stars in their yellow three-wheeler, flashing the word Amma in red and blue, red and blue. An appreciative aah! rose up from the audience. The wisdom of the red-and-blue colour scheme was now abundantly clear.

When the stars stepped out the crowd fell silent in wonderment. They had known Viraj from his baby days when he ran around pot-bellied and naked, pissing in every puddle. But the local boy had grown up and made good, and was bringing home his white beloved.

And what a beloved! In her white Stetson, blue jeans and red plaid shirt (oh, those colours!) she stood a head taller than him, and looked just like the lead singer of—what was that group again, that was on TV last week?—the Cosmic Gays.

The men in the white van watched from the shadows.

They took in the fairy lights and the arrival of the happy couple, one of whom was their intended victim. Kidnap, extortion and murder is one thing. Love and marriage another. It would be almost indecent for one to intrude upon the other. Goons they may have been, but they had their manners, their codes of honour and conduct. The nobbling of Viraj would have to wait. Turning their van round they went home to their wives, full of the joys of romance and Bollywood.

When Viraj entered his humble home with Debs on his arm, a sigh arose from the relatives lining the walls.

'What a great broadside of beef!' murmured his grandma appreciatively. In a society that measured bride-price by the pound, Viraj was bringing home a king's ransom.

'He'd better watch his step,' said Viraj's Dad proudly. 'She'll snap his neck off if he steps out of line.'

'That's not all she'll snap,' said the grandma, who had been at the arrack long before the party began.

At the nakath time, they lit the ceremonial oil lamp. How quaint, thought Debs. All this to-do for a private family dinner.

Viraj pulled out two rings. He slipped one on her finger. Gold!

But by now Debs was beginning to sense that something was badly wrong.

'Now you put this ring on me,' instructed Viraj.

'No,' she said with horror. 'Viraj, no!'

The full meaning of it all became clear when she looked round at the assembled company, their expectant faces.

She smiled grimly, a smile full of tombstone teeth.

'It's been nice knowing you, folks!' she said and bounded out of there in the best traditions of the Western, hatless and horseless. She ran as fast as her long legs would carry her and when she reached the cemetery wall she vaulted over in one easy sweep. She ran without stopping till she hit the chapel of rest.

When Lenin Marx Siddhu finally opened one eye he saw a large moon face yawing over him, ghostly white with tombstone teeth.

'Well, hello there!' it said.

Terror leant fresh strength to his legs. He sprang up with a shriek and ran into the darkening night.

The guests at the betrothal found to their surprise that disappointment had not dulled their appetite. Nothing is more consoling than someone else's misfortune, and misery is the best tonic of all just as long as it's not your own. The guests ate every last scrap of food and went their way.

Viraj's mum found him alone under the banana tree, smoking; his first cigarette in over a year.

'I can't understand it. She really liked me.'

His mother put her arm around him. Twenty-five he may have been, but he was still her son.

'Never mind,' she said. 'There'll be others.'

Neither could comprehend what had actually happened. If a girl put her hand familiarly on you and said 'Machang', that was surely tantamount to saying, 'I want to go to bed with you.'

But nice girls of their class didn't have sex. They had babies. So the only way forward was an engagement. (Sex before marriage was only practised by the corrupt upper classes of Colombo Seven.) If you had to have it, if it was virtually a medical necessity, you did the decent thing and went to a comfort woman like Celestina on the next lane. By paying good money for it you absolved yourself of any wrongdoing. But sex for the sheer fun of it? The thought was almost too obscene for words.

16

The two sisters, Mrs Herath and Mrs Rodrigo, met for round two of their discussions, this time in Deal Place. The narrow road was clogged with ministerial security, armoured cars, armed guards and white-gloved outriders. Especially during election time, Mrs Rodrigo was a precious commodity in the eyes of the outside world. One of these days, she vowed, I'm going to shock them all by travelling alone, incognito, in a three-wheeler. But then nobody would know about it and the whole point of the exercise would be lost. Forget that.

'We have to plan this like a military campaign, Evangeline, we only get one crack at it.'

'What news of the enemy?'

The enemy was that one person capable of upsetting their carefully laid plans, the strange girl who turned up at Deal Place every now and then. Dulcie had told Evangeline all about her. She was the dog in the manger, the cuckoo in the nest, the fly in the ointment. (Mrs Herath liked to mix her metaphors as thoroughly as her acharu. It brought out the flavours, she said.)

'You know they went down south for the weekend? Together.'

'Disgusting,' said Mrs Rodrigo with more than a hint of regret. 'What sort of parents has he got?'

'The father's dead, I think. And the mother . . . I don't know how I can bring myself to tell you this, and I sincerely hope it won't put you off . . .' She went into Marek's room, rooted about in his belongings and came out with the naughty postcard.

'Outrageous!' muttered Mrs Rodrigo. 'Imagine having that as the mother-in-law of my daughter.'

'It's a good thing she's abroad.'

'She obviously is. The postcard says it all.'

And so the planning continued. It was going to be a small select lunch party (you could even call it exclooziv) to be held at the Herath residence in Deal Place. No point scaring the young man prematurely with obelisks and polar bears.

'I will get you some private caterers,' said Mrs Rodrigo.

'What's wrong with my cooking?'

'Ranjith uses them all the time for his constituency affairs. Fuk-a-Luk Fine Dining. They're absolutely marvellous.'

Piyumi dialled her mother. I'll give it one last try, she thought.

'Ma, you wouldn't want to sell one of the flats and let me bring the money out here to buy Serendipity, would you?'

'Oh, absolutely. Just ask Mrs Rodrigo if there's room under the bed for both of us.'

'I'll take that as a no, then?'

'Piyumi. Darling. Listen to me. Every day I read about election incidents over there. It's only a matter of time before the whole place goes up in flames again. What idiot would want to buy at a time like this?' She paused, then answered her own question. 'You, I suppose. By the way, Guy called.'

'Guy?'

'Your boss, remember? He needs desperately to speak to you.'

So Piyumi put the phone down and dialled Guy Boyd-Maunsell, QC, Head of Chambers.

'I'm so glad you rang, Miss, Miss . . .'

I have a first name, Piyumi said silently into the phone, you've used it before, don't be afraid.

'Miss Segarajasingham. I finally got the Sri Lankan number from your mother. It wasn't easy, I tell you!'

She could picture him twirling and twisting the long strand of hair by his ear. Then he would paste it on top where the bald patch was.

'But every time I dial some idiot hangs up on me.'

'Suranganee.'

'What's that? Anyway the thing is, we need you to take a decision. It's been almost a month now and we're really missing your expertise.'

Liar, thought Piyumi, you're dying to get rid of me. 'I'll let you know,' she said out loud. 'Thanks, Guy.'

Who would have thought even a month ago it would come to this? A change of countries, careers, partners. (Well, maybe not partners, not yet.) Her decision seemed almost inevitable.

She had slung the gallon of petrol all over the bridge. It only remained for her to toss a lighted match on it.

The opposition parliamentarians met in their turn, a much smaller gathering at a more modest venue, not a five-star hotel.

'They're pulling ahead. All the polls show them in the lead,' reported their spokesman.

'The problem,' said the opposition leader gloomily, 'is that they look poor and we look rich. If you look poor, the people automatically assume you've got millions stashed away in a Swiss bank account. So they love and respect you. On the other hand, if you look rich,' he sighed, 'they know you're operating on a thundering overdraft. They have no respect for you whatsoever.

'That's why we're here at the Fuk-a-Luk Café and not at the Hilton.'

'Their candidate, Rodrigo. He's the hot favourite. He's zooming ahead in the polls.'

'My point entirely. Man looks like a pauper, the people adore him. But he's rich, rich, rich. I happen to know he keeps polar bears for pets.'

'He's worked wonders for the people. During his time at the ministry, he's almost single-handedly eliminated diphtheria, whooping cough and newspaper editors.'

'Remarkable.'

'And you should see the garbage mountain at Bloemendahl. Imagine how prosperous people must be if they can afford to throw away so much!'

'To come back to our agenda,' said the leader, 'I want to stress, from now on, no trousers. Trousers are decadent, trousers are rich. I realize you like to wear them in the privacy of your own homes, but when you go out, please desist. It has to be sarong and sandals.'

'Can I wear my hil-hil vest with the sarong?'

'Certainly not, that's almost bordering on the obscene. There's a limit to one's poverty.'

The leader put on his spectacles and opened the menu. 'Now who's for the chicken and sweet corn, who's for the prawn balls? Oh by the way, I can really recommend the chilli paste here.'

At school, too, the political arguments raged.

'When we get in,' said Somawathie, 'it'll be back to traditional values. There'll be no miniskirts.'

'If you get in,' said Iresha. Though on opposite sides of the political divide they had become firm friends. 'Anyway, how are you going to stop me?'

'We'll have crack teams of modesty police patrolling the streets. They'll arrest you.'

'They'll have to take down my particulars. They won't be able to resist.'

'Yes,' sighed Somawathie. 'That's what I am afraid of.' They went back to the far more pressing question of what they were going to do for the end of term fund-raiser concert.

The first clouds of spring scudded across the sky, blown this way and that by the wind, as Marek's mother toiled up High Street. She had taken to meeting Dennis Ridoynauth after work every day at his offices on Clapham Common, where they walked about a bit before returning home. The journey back was easier because it was downhill. After many years in her room she was beginning to find that outside wasn't as bad as all that. In fact, Margate had been glorious.

A tall courtly man in a cashmere coat and soft felt hat stood before her.

'Guava juice,' he said.

She stared at him for a moment uncomprehendingly.

'It's my guava juice you're fond of.'

She shook her head. 'I stopped drinking guava juice months ago.'

'I hear your son is well.'

'I don't have a son,' she began. Then she remembered.

'I see he's gone south for the weekend with his girlfriend.'

'Girlfriend?' She laughed loudly, almost in relief. 'You've got the wrong bloke, mate. My Marek doesn't do girlfriends.'

But the stranger had vanished into one of the shops on High Street, leaving her to wonder about this curious world outside where total strangers stopped you on street corners and made weird remarks about your children.

17

The day the ad appeared, Suranganee had the best time of all, marshalling and directing the marauding invaders. 'Not there, not on that ebony sofa! Move along, move along there please!'

When one particularly buxom matron asked why on earth she shouldn't sit on the ebony sofa, Suranganee replied sweetly, 'Because, Madam, you're fat.'

'How dare you! I'm not fat!'

'No,' said Suranganee thoughtfully. 'I suppose not. You're enormous.'

The woman took this in good spirit. It was worth enduring any insult from the staff just to look, listen and learn about how the other half lived. And my goodness, it was turning out to be such an eye-opener. Life without a flat screen TV, imagine! And these rickety bits of furniture you wouldn't even consider having in your back kitchen, with bugs in the rattan biting your backside. And those moth-eaten, dog-bitten bits of rug they called carpets! Where, oh where, was the oatmeal wall-to-wall Wilton?

Then there were the strong silent types who wandered

round casing the joint, in white bush shirts and heavy gold watches straight off the pavements of Pettah. If this were a Bollywood film they would have been the goons of some minister. And this is indeed what they were, a clear example of life imitating art.

'If you have nothing to do, don't do it here!' said Suranganee, or words to that effect. The goons didn't understand English but they certainly understood Suranganee.

With two firm offers on the table the fuss had died down somewhat, but the energy of those ravenous hordes seemed somehow to have transferred to the normally lethargic inhabitants of Serendipity. You could almost see little sparks of electricity in their red eyes, you could imagine their hair bristling with electrons: the risen dead supercharged and walking again.

Piyumi who had missed out, having been away, felt strangely out of place and untouched by it all. The talk was all of Nizam now, Nizam this and Nizam that. 'As Nizam said to me,' was the preface to many a statement, or 'Just imagine what Nizam will make of this.' Nizam was one of the firm buyers, the purveyor of steel and glass palaces to the rich and famous. Small and portly and self-effacing, he had red, almost hairless cheeks and a straggling beard below the jaw line. He got on with people: you could see how he had made a success of his business.

Piyumi tried remonstrating with him. 'You'll let me keep my bit, won't you? The bit with the pavilion? Or even a piece of the main house. I'm not fussy!'

He listened in silence to her long tale about how historic

houses were converted nowadays, preserving the outside but with clever modernization within. Then he shrugged.

'It's not what people want.'

And there you had it. He was not in the business of educating people about what they should and should not want. He was in the business of giving them what they did want, now. (And earning himself a fortune in the process.) If people decided twenty years down the line that they might have preferred the old house after all, it would be too late. But that was not his problem nor his fault. In the meantime he was sorry, he really couldn't let her keep a piece —it would get in the way of the development and he needed every square inch to make this project worthwhile.

Nizam smiled his charming, self-deprecating smile and went about his business of measuring and surveying and getting estimates for demolition. Privately he realized you could build at least four good houses with the material from this one. It was the ancient story of new lamps for old.

Piyumi wandered from room to room in a daze. She was like the old woman searching high and low for something, she couldn't remember what; telling and retelling her beads though she had long forgotten the meaning of the prayer. The short-term memory was gone, though in her case there had never been much of a long-term one either. She had left the country too young to carry any of the heavy baggage of horror and unhappiness many others had carried. For her it had been a move like any other, an adventure, because when you're young you don't live for today or even tomorrow; you live for the day after that.

There was a history here she felt compelled to memorize and re-memorize. An essence she had to capture and put into a bottle, to be used sparingly in years to come. But she had no conscious idea why or what this was. She began to pack her bags.

'Leaving so soon?' Suranganee asked sweetly when she met her on the landing with her suitcase.

'I'm moving into the pavilion.' Leaving Suranganee open-mouthed on the stairs she made her weary way down.

Nizam was having his lawyers inspect the deeds. He was buying for cash: the deal would be complete in a matter of weeks. A few weeks is better than nothing, she thought. Let me enjoy my smallholding for the last few weeks.

When Viraj dropped Marek off that evening, she got them to lug the iron bed all the way downstairs into the pavilion. The almirah was too heavy to shift: you'd need a *baas* to dismantle and re-assemble it.

'Where are you going to store your clothes?' Marek asked, but it was Viraj who answered, 'You string a line from one end of the room to the other, and you hang everything on it.' That was what they did in the watte.

Viraj was looking round for that very pretty girl in the pink dress who opened the gates to him every day but she was nowhere to be seen. Debs had let him down so badly his ego was bruised, his confidence shattered. A little fling with the pink dress is what I need to set me to rights. Two weeks with me and she's mine forever, he thought somewhat philosophically. As it happened, fate or serendipity or whatever it was, had other plans for him.

Holed up in the high wide rooms to the right of the first floor landing—the best rooms in the house—Suranganee and Ganga watched the proceedings through the adjustable teak louvres of the double doors.

'Disgraceful!' Ganga muttered. 'She's started bringing three-wheeler kariars into the house now!'

Just then the iron bed floated across their line of vision, passing uncomfortably close to their noses, and with a sibilant hiss, Ganga snapped the louvres shut.

After her little misadventure, Debs found herself making excuses every afternoon for not going to the gym. Her staff were mystified. The apparently never-ending stream of official meetings and business courtesy calls suddenly seemed to have dried up. When she did finally go, almost a week later, Viraj avoided her gaze. By mutual consent they stuck to different ends of the gym. When, accidentally, they both reached out for the same fifteen-kilo weight, they were scrupulously civil with each other.

'Go on, have it.'

'No, you have it.'

'I can wait, you go ahead.'

'Take it!' bellowed Debs, and immediately regretted her outburst. Looking round, she realized that everyone knew what had happened the other night. Her flight had been witnessed by half-a-hundred people in the watte.

Miraculously, her popularity, rather than diminishing, had zoomed: she was the prize that had unaccountably slipped through Viraj's fingers; now everyone else wanted a piece of the action.

But Debs herself had had enough. Enough of men, those tricky creatures with their subliminal desires, half-expressed, half-suppressed. They came over all friendly one minute, and next minute their hand was down your T-shirt groping your tits. It's women only for me from now on, she vowed, I'll never complain about women again.

So it was something of a bolt from heaven, therefore, when she got a call from Piyumi.

'I'm in want,' said Piyumi. 'In want of a job.'

Debs's heart leapt. But she had a roomful of women observing her closely, in front of whom she had to behave.

'What are your skills?' she asked cautiously.

'I'm a barrister. You know that.'

'Briefs? Hmm, interesting. You'll have to come in for an interview, of course.'

'Anything,' said Piyumi. 'Anything.'

'I'll have to vet you thoroughly. We have strict guidelines about this sort of thing.'

'I was afraid you'd say that,' said Piyumi tonelessly.

After putting the phone down, Debs wanted to erupt from her cubicle in a song and dance routine. 'There is nothing like a dame!' she wanted to shout. She restrained herself with difficulty. There were others in the room, watching in want.

Marek's heart broke when he saw Piyumi sitting on the iron bed with a length of coir rope strung across the room, displaying the meagre contents of her suitcase for all the world to see. It reminded him of that other time: his whole life seemed to consist of packing and repacking her clothes. With her bright eyes and show of defiance she looked like some small animal retired to its lair, knowing it is about to die. He couldn't see himself being so brave in the face of adversity. He would have taken the first flight back. I have to help her, he thought. I'm all she has.

When he got home to Deal Place, the Heraths were watching their brother-in-law on TV at yet another election rally.

'When we took over,' he was roaring, 'this country was on the absolute brink of disaster. Since then, I think you'll all agree, we have taken a decisive step forward!'

'Jaya Wewa!' roared the crowd.

Wordlessly, Mrs Herath handed Marek yet another postcard and he saw that serendipity had struck again.

'Dennis wants me to move in with him into the downstairs flat. I've told him I'll think about it. He wants me to go to Granada with him. Wants wants wants. What do I do with our flat? Sell?'

'Not bad news, I hope?' asked Mrs Herath hopefully. She had in fact read and re-read the postcard and pondered its contents all day. She had discussed it at length with Evangeline over the telephone. Mr Herath had heard nothing all day but postcard, postcard, postcard.

He was sick to death of it.

'Can I use your telephone?' Marek asked. 'It's an abroad call. I'll pay.'

'Please,' said Mrs Herath. 'Go right ahead.'

She retired behind a large potted palm so she could listen better.

'Ma, it's me.'

'How're you there? All right?'

She sounded preoccupied, Marek thought, as if her attention was taken up elsewhere. She was, in fact, giving Dennis a head massage at that moment.

'Maybe you should sell the flat and send me the money out here.'

There was silence. 'It's that girlfriend of yours, isn't it?'

How news travels! he thought in wonderment. Or has she been at the tarot again?

'Girlfriend? What girlfriend?'

She laughed. 'You're my son, remember? There's not much about you I don't know.'

As if, he thought. As if.

'Marek,' she said earnestly. 'You're a rich boy. They'll always be after your money, remember that.'

'Will you at least think about it?'

'It's the worst idea you ever had. But I'll think about it.' She laughed again. 'If you like.'

Mrs Herath reappeared from behind the potted palm refreshed by all this new information and disquieted at the same time. It was plain she and Evangeline would have to act quickly.

'Are you in next Sunday?'

'Yes,' he replied mechanically. 'Why?'

'Oh, nothing. My sister might drop in, that's why. That was her husband on TV just now. You know, he's contesting.'

But Marek was lost in thought. He went into his room shutting the door behind him.

Almost at the same time another call was being put through from Sri Lanka to England. Mr Skanda picked up the phone behind the fridge.

'They're on to us,' said the voice at the other end of the phone. 'We'll have to bring the date forward.'

'We can't. It's not up to us.' The voice continued talking.

'Don't panic,' said Mr Skanda. 'It's important not to panic.'

18

The elections were planned to take place just before the Sri Lankan New Year. This was not to aid the general public so much as politicians themselves, who would be sent off after their labours to relax at an appropriate venue. If you had been especially successful you were dispatched to the steamy fleshpots of Bangkok. Otherwise, it was the cool climes of Nuwara Eliya for you, where you wore flat caps and played golf and generally behaved in a dated thirties' manner. Yet others preferred to observe the wildlife in Yala: so much more tame than your own wild life back in Colombo (though it was always enjoyable and instructive to watch other predators in action). Anything, really, but the Eco-lodge in Anuradhapura. This was where you were posted if you had only scraped through with a wafer-thin majority.Here you survived without electricity, washing your clothes in the stream with Sunlight soap, brushing your teeth with charcoal and generally having a miserable time and pretending you loved it because—ah!—at last you were at one with your own people. If the mosquitoes didn't get you, the Tigers probably would. If you survived, you generally came back a broken man.

Evangeline Rodrigo wasn't going anywhere. New York or nothing, she had told her husband, and since New York was too far, they would stay put. She had high hopes that after elections the minister was destined for greater things than mere 'infernal affairs'. He was giving a big rally at the stadium just before election day. Nobody in the party could pull in crowds like he could. And he'll need me then, she thought grimly. There may be any number of interns. There is only one Wife.

The inhabitants of Serendipity weren't going anywhere either, but only because they couldn't afford it. There was a sort of über-snobbery about this. Their grandfather had once owned a magnificent bungalow up in Nuwara Eliya, long since sold. Nowadays, Nuwara Eliya belonged to the riff-raff with their poxy, boxy Swiss chalets and their tiny, shiny techno-Japanese lodges.

Anyway, it was the perfect time of year for Colombo Seven. The streets with their giant flowering trees were suddenly empty of people and you could actually hear the birds sing; and you were back in time twenty years when the parapet walls to these houses were just waist-high and the only sign of life on the streets was the occasional lottery ticket seller, or a man shouldering an enormous gunny sack of oysters for sale. And the oysters were not for eating, of course, but for the occasional pearl you might find, which was better than any lottery ticket.

Only one thing marred this peace: the threatened lack of

staff. At New Year, everyone wanted a minimum of two weeks off. Two weeks without bread, milk and newspapers was bad enough; two weeks without a kitchen maid was a plain insult.

Every New Year the cook left for almost a month: it was only fair since she never went anywhere the rest of the year. This left Suranganee who was, as always, open to negotiation.

She would begin with her opening gambit.

'My sister's getting married. I may have to leave a little early this year.'

'People don't get married at New Year,' Ganga would retort sharply. 'Besides, I didn't know you had a sister.'

'She's my cousin-brother's sister-in-law's eldest uncle's middle daughter.'

'Very close then.'

'I promised to be there to help with the sheets.'

'Sheets?'

'You know. The morning after. Duh!' She didn't actually say duh! but she meant it.

If Ganga was shocked that in the village they still inspected nuptial sheets the morning after, she had the good sense not to show it. With Suranganee you never knew. She might even have been telling the truth.

'Of course if I send them a very good present . . .'

Ganga saw her opening and seized it. 'What present?'

'That sari you wore for the Aluwihare wedding?'

Ganga was speechless. 'That's a Benaresi! Those threads are dipped in pure gold!'

Suranganee concentrated her attentions on a dust ball that had got stuck on the bedspread.

She flicked it experimentally.

'You can have that very smart blue nylon I got in Madras.'

'Nylon?' asked Suranganee. 'Nylon?' Her voice was thin, the question rhetorical. She didn't expect a reply.

'Then the red-and-white candy stripe Piyumi's mother sent me from London.'

'I remember when you got that,' said Suranganee dreamily. 'You said the woman must be blind. You said you'd wear it the day you got a job outside a barbershop, turning round and round like a pole.'

Suranganee paused a moment. Then she said, almost indistinctly, 'Barefoot.'

'Barefoot?'

'Barefoot. The orange and pink silk from Barefoot.' Ganga knew when she was beaten. Imagine! The lower classes demanding silk sarees from Barefoot! Why didn't they ask for cake? So much easier and a whole lot less expensive.

Piyumi summoned an emergency council of war to discuss the Serendipity Question, as she had taken to calling it. She had hoped for Uncle Bala's attendance, Bala being the only Segarajasingham whose sympathies might have leant towards hers, but he had cried off.

'Your Aunty Pushpam and I need the money,' he said simply. 'A small two-bed flat will do for us. We want to visit the Holy Land, the Masai Mara, the temples of Pagan.' He had it all planned, she could see it in his eyes; the plans didn't include Serendipity. So it was down to a council of two: she and Marek on the iron bed.

There was no more painting. All that seemed irrelevant now. For Piyumi it had been a way of staking her claim on the property, like a dog marking out its territory. There was no need now, she was in possession. It was a quixotic last stand: it wouldn't be long before the invaders arrived.

That year the rains came early, well before New Year. The colonial powers in their wisdom had built Colombo on a swamp, cutting a sophisticated network of canals through the town, dredging and draining the land in between. In the intervening half-millennium, developers had filled in the canals, building on every bit of low-lying land they could lay their hands on, filling in the spaces like a giant jig-saw. But they reckoned without the power of nature. Any tropical storm and nature reclaimed her own, turning Colombo into a lake once more, dotted by tiny islands of houses, the older ones built on higher bits of land remaining relatively untouched.

The minister of housing, who had developed a large tract of land to the east of the town centre, found himself having to visit his tenants by boat. On the whole he managed to collect more abuse than rent. Ganga's best friend, an elderly Colpetty lady, took refuge on top of an almirah, clutching her pet Pekinese to her bosom.

It was only five in the evening, but the sky was already black. Viraj drove the three-wheeler all the way to the pavilion at the back. He had said hi to the girl at the gates but she appeared not to hear. He knew the storm would be violent, and decided to wait it out because the three-wheeler wouldn't be able to cope in the rain. He spent the time doing push-ups on the small verandah of the pavilion. There was no sign of the girl in the pink dress. He had visions of her running towards him through the rain, hair loose and arms outstretched in the best Bollywood tradition, singing a Hindi song in a high-pitched nasal voice. Of course, the rain would have pasted the dress to her body making it totally see-through. The image of this was almost too much to bear, and Viraj did a few more furious press-ups to keep himself pure.

As Marek entered the pavilion, the trip switch went, plunging it into darkness. The first fat, delicious drops of rain began to fall, releasing a perfume of scorched earth and wilted jasmine. The darkness leant a curious air of intimacy to the two of them as they sat on the bed, an unexpected clarity to their thoughts.

'We're both alike,' he was saying. 'We're both single children, we both have controlling mothers. We are essentially all alone in this world.' And that is why we should team up, he wanted to add, but just then the lightning flashed on their faces and he lost courage.

She shook her head. 'I actually think we are diametric opposites. Your religion instructs you to weigh the pros and cons, the good and bad every step of the way, but you're the least bothered by all that. You're quite happy to take things lying down.'

'Lying down? I like that! Here I am, trying to sort your problems out when it's actually nothing to do with me, and this is all the thanks I get.'

'But you have ulterior motives,' she said cunningly. There was a sudden waft of jasmine through the open door as if someone had just walked in. Both looked up, but all they could see were the intermittent flashes, grey and silver and black, lighting up the garden like an old photograph.

She continued, 'I, on the other hand, who ought to believe in the music of the stars, the divine patterns of action and reaction, am forced every step of the way to take a proactive stance.' She sighed. 'And nothing's going the way I want.'

'My mother might sell our flat.'

'No,' she said, a little too quickly, and saw him wince. She put a hand on his arm. 'I mean I have one last card to play. I can't talk about it yet but you'll be the first to know if it works out.'

They sat in silence listening to the rain, together but apart. Almost married, almost not.

For weeks they had been talking of nothing at the Mogambo International but the forthcoming fund-raiser concert. Everybody had been given the day off to practise. Percy ffinch-Percy took Marek with him from class to class on a tour of inspection.

Form Two had got up quite a wind ensemble and were farting away merrily when ffinch-Percy opened their door.

'Morning Mr ffinch-Percy!'

'Morning, class! Who's been at the lentils then?'

He closed the door and clutched his stomach. 'Ooh, where are my antacid pills?' he asked tragically.

Form Three were practising the National Anthem. They listened outside for a moment.

'Perfect,' said Percy. 'At least they can't go far wrong with that.' He began singing along. 'No more, no more, no more, Martha-a-a . . .'

'Martha's my ex-wife,' he explained. 'Those days I used to sing this to her every night. But would she listen?' he added sadly.

Further down the corridor, there were loud shrieks emanating from Form Four. Inside they saw a woman in shiny satin, a curry-yellow ball gown. Mrs Leelaratne.

'I'm giving myself a dress rehearsal,' she explained. 'Strauss's "Four Last Songs".'

'Marvellous,' said ffinch-Percy. 'Marvellous.'

He closed the door. 'Really,' he said to Marek. 'I'm not surprised those were his four last songs. I hope they shot him after that.'

Inside the Form Five classroom Fernando was showing a young mother the basic movements of the pasa doble. At least that's what they hoped it was. Mr ffinch-Percy quickly shut the door on them.

'There'll be trouble one of these days if I don't put him back on the gates,' he muttered darkly. 'Trouble is, he's made ICT so popular I'm not sure I can afford to replace him.'

Marek's own class had almost unilaterally decided on a fashion show because most of the girls fancied their chances on the ramp. Princy's designer friend Rafaelo would be showing his collection of saris.

'Of course he'll be bringing his own models. Very fussy about who wears his saris, is Raf. You have to be stick thin and six feet tall.'

'That rules out most of Colombo then.'

'The good thing,' said Percy ffinch-Percy rubbing his hands gleefully, 'is that every politician will bring his own fleet of vehicles. Nothing impresses a prospective parent more than Monteros and Pajeros. They are the very symbols of international school success.'

'We have to go out and celebrate,' said Debs, 'the success of your job application.'

'Where are we going?' Piyumi watched the corded muscles of Viraj's back through the thin wife-beater T-shirt he was wearing. Why can't he fancy me? she thought unhappily. The tuk-tuk stopped outside the Gallery Café, Debs's favourite watering hole.

'Wait here for us,' said Debs with her charming tombstone smile. She had forgiven Viraj his trespasses of the other night. Indeed, she had wholeheartedly forgiven him for being a man, which was essentially his problem. What Viraj felt about it all wasn't clear. Not even to himself. He found he still burned with a desire to be close to her. But was this desire emotional or sexual? He would have waited outside the Gallery Café for a month if she had asked him to.

'Waiter, two strawberry mojitos over here,' said Debs.

She turned to Piyumi. 'You'll find us a jolly bunch of girls. Foreign NGOs are much maligned. We always get the rough end of the stick.' She guffawed and put a calloused hand on Piyumi's neck.

'Did I tell you about the ghost I saw the other night? I happened to be jogging in the cemetery. There's a pretty little chapel there and I'd just stopped to get my breath. The ghost had silvery hair and a pointy silvery beard. It sprang at my throat with a shriek but I stood my ground, you know me. It gibbered viciously at me and ran away.'

Three mojitos each later and they piled back into the three-wheeler. 'Home,' said Debs expansively. They came to a stop outside a large block of flats.

Piyumi opened her eyes. 'This is not Serendipity,' she declared and promptly closed her eyes again.

'The last part of your interview,' whispered Debs moistly. 'The final test.'

Piyumi found herself in the lift shooting up to the thirty-fourth floor. She could feel Debs's hot breath on the back of her neck. She had a vague idea of what was in store.

Oh well, she thought, easier to give in than resist. The story of my life. Anyway, this is probably written in the stars too. These days she was having to shut her eyes and think of Serendipity an awful lot.

19

'You will go into the office on your own,' Debs told her over the orange juice next morning. 'We will not let our love intrude upon our work.'

'What love?' Piyumi wanted to ask but didn't for fear of getting the sack. In the event, she needn't have worried.

After the juice and two pieces of very dry kurakkan toast with passion jam ('No butter,' said Debs, 'absolutely not!') Piyumi took herself off home in a strange three-wheeler. The young cop at the roadblock raised an eyebrow at her dishevelled state. Feeling too fragile to fight back she gave him her widest, sweetest smile. He waved her through.

Back at Serendipity she showered and changed, putting on her most barristerial clothes. Catching sight of herself in a scrap of mirror she felt suddenly, unaccountably, happy. She was in her own home in the country of her choice, setting out to work at a normal everyday job at a normal everyday hour: the sun shone on her and at that moment she could have saved the world; even if she couldn't save Serendipity. Maybe, she thought, this is the secret of life, to go from one moment of unalloyed happiness to the next, leaving out the many sadnesses in between. If you could stitch together a past composed entirely of these moments you would surely die fulfilled and happy.

The young cop was even more surprised this time round. He let out a long low whistle as she drove through. She gave him a limp two-fingered wave. Her Queen-at-Ascot wave.

In the Fort area she quickly realized the folly of bringing a car in. There was nowhere to park. Driving round and round the offices she finally managed to squeeze into a tiny space in front of a kade selling coffee and pastries in a side alley. The owner came rushing out to berate her for blocking his entrance. To appease him, she bought four plump malu pan hot from the oven, stuffed with fish curry. He gave her a dirty look, he wasn't impressed. So she bought a serving of dhal with a half-loaf of bread. Still no improvement. Going for broke she bought the entire remains of a tray of very old, very stale onion sambal. She could see the beginnings of a smile on his face. Before he could commend her for her bravery, she paid and fled. I'll have the malu pan for lunch she thought, ditching the rest in the bin by the lift.

In the office, Debs treated her with a sort of strict professionalism she neither expected nor deserved. It was amazing how Debs could so easily compartmentalize heart and head: Piyumi was still enough of a Sri Lankan to find this almost impossible. Hey! she wanted to shout at many points throughout the day, aren't I the girl you've just been to bed with? Don't I deserve a little respect around here, a little tender loving care? But she was caught, because this wasn't actually what she wanted: she only wanted to be offered it so she could graciously refuse. Thanks, but no thanks.

The Women in Want were not at all what she had been led to expect either. They were actually a very nice, strangely normal bunch of Sri Lankans attempting vainly to navigate the mystifying world of NGO-dom, to tackle the curiously unintelligible argot of NGO-speak. There were certain golden rules which Piyumi quickly mastered:

*Never say in one sentence what you can possibly say in five.

*If you're asked to write a report, it must never be less than 300 pages long.

*The report must at all times be accompanied by indices, appendices, addenda, errata, epilogues, prologues and just plain logues (though these are optional).

*Don't worry if you can't understand it because nobody else will either. They certainly won't read it because everybody in this world understands perfectly well your report is only a totem, a potent fetish, a ju-ju, to be kept in front of you at conferences and passed round from hand to hand with reverence. If just once in your lifetime, your report becomes miraculously transubstantiated into action then you are indeed truly blessed.

Piyumi longed for the day she would be called upon to write such a text.

There were three Sri Lankan women in the office. Sharmila, with her many years of experience in foreign organizations, was well versed in the arcane arts of NGO. She was also tri-lingual (Sinhalese, English, NGO-speak). There was Janaki, the good-natured one who did most of the work. And finally Cassandra—Cassie—who, contrary to expectations, was the optimistic one, seeing great hope for women of the country. Sri Lanka had very high female literacy, low infant mortality and a female life-expectancy that was the envy of every South Asian country. It had also had the world's first woman prime minister twenty years back. There had been little progress since.

Surprisingly, there were Men in Want too, just two of them, occupying lowly positions in the office. There was the junior assistant (for which read peon) and there was the technician. The technician was basically the man who ran upstairs and complained whenever the lights went out, the AC began to drip on unsuspecting visitors, or the washbasin got blocked. The office was sub-let by Bilious and Dicey upstairs, and Asian landlords generally responded better to men. At the start, when things went wrong Debs had gone herself, throwing her not inconsiderable weight around: they had been so terrified of her up there at Bilious that it had paralysed them into inaction. That was when Debs had reluctantly acknowledged the necessity of Premachandra who, though puny and shrill, was essentially still a man, and managed to wheedle the landlords into getting whatever it was repaired.

At three every afternoon Debs came out of her cubicle and clapped her hands. 'Girls!' she said. 'I need not remind you how far we have to go.'

Then she went. To her gym, which was not as far as all that, just down the Galle Road. That was when the real work of the day began, the typing of reports, the rehashing of politics and the doings of rent-a-crowd. Piyumi was a welcome addition. She knew hardly anyone so was less likely to contradict the more juicy bits of gossip flying around town. Besides, her spelling was impeccable and she could proof-read any report.

At lunchtime she shared her malu pan with the girls. Debs ate on her own in her cubicle, dining lightly on a blue cheese, walnut and rocket salad.

'You'll get fat!' she bellowed through the glass when she saw the buns.

The dynamics of Debs's love greatly interested Piyumi even if the love itself didn't. They were very much the dynamics of power and patronage, even, dare she admit, of master and servant: I'll tell you what's good for you because I know you don't know any better. Besides, you love it when I tell you what to do, you know you do!

Do I? thought Piyumi belligerently. Do I, heck!

Debs had chosen to bestow her love much as a world body might choose to give a poor country a loan. It was supposed to command instant love and admiration and, of course, undying allegiance. And just as the world body, flushed with the beneficence and self-importance of its gesture, might move on to new countries immediately thereafter, so Piyumi could see the searchlight of Debs's love move on. It happened within days. Thank God, Piyumi thought. I'm not cut out to be at the receiving end of too much these days.

Your love for me is like an IMF loan, she wanted to sing. Benevolent and unconditional it may be. It carries for me zero interest.

Marek was woken up early Sunday morning by the sounds of scaffolding going up outside his bedroom window. The potatoes in his mattress had been particularly hard and unyielding last night. Turning over he burrowed in between the lumps and closed his eyes again.

Outside, it was all action with both Heraths in attendance. The workmen had planted four galvanized iron poles into Mr Herath's precious front lawn and were bolting together the cross-pieces. The corrugated iron sheets that were to go on top lay in a heap on the ground. 'It's only a takarang shed!' said Mr Herath, bewildered.

'It's a marquee,' corrected Mrs Herath. 'They'll be covering it with coconut thatch once they've finished.'

'Whose damn fool idea was that?'

'Evangeline's. She likes a rustic ambience.'

'It'll look like a cowshed.'

'Are you calling my sister a cow?'

A black van arrived, with gold lettering on the outside which said Fuk-a-Luk Fine Dining.

The driver parked and jumped down. A moment later he had put on a tall white hat transforming himself almost instantly into a chef. He opened the double doors at the back with a flourish to reveal a stack of clay pots; also an elderly wall-eyed waiter. The clay pots were all empty. (The waiter looked pretty vacant too.) The food for the event had actually been cooked under hygienic stainless steel conditions back at the café. It was to be transferred to clay pots at the last minute so guests could get the benefit of real village cooking. The minister particularly required it. It looked good in the pictures, he said.

'Who's paying for all this?'

'Certainly not you. That's for sure.'

'Where's the boy?'

'Still asleep.'

At that moment the boy appeared, mug of coffee in hand, just inside the front door. He couldn't immediately take in what looked to him like a slightly surreal village scene from a pantomime: the thatched hut, the aproned chef, the wall-eyed waiter.

'Think I'll go out for a bit,' he said sleepily.

'No, you won't.' Mrs Herath moved smartly to block his exit.

'She's the boss,' said Mr Herath acting for once in concert with his wife. He winked.

'I promised to meet someone,' explained Marek.

That dreadful girl again, out to ruin everything! Out loud Mrs Herath said, 'My sister's coming round. She's dying to meet you.'

'Oh.' Marek disappeared back inside.

'You haven't told him?' Mr Herath asked his wife in disbelief.

'The less he knows the better. That's the absolute essence of a successful marriage. Take it from me.'

'I did,' said Mr Herath. 'Remember?'

Deal Place was beginning to fill up with security. There were as yet no VIPs but the narrow street was already crowded with plainclothes men lounging about with studied indifference, picking their nose, picking their zits, scratching their armpits and other places. They were all aged between twenty and thirty.

In the chummery down at the bottom of the road, Raf had arrived with his models for a practice run-through of his fashion show. But Princy and Percy ffinch-Percy were upstairs watching the street. They found this view far more interesting.

'I want that one,' said Princy. 'I want that one and that one.'

'I want that one, that one, that one and that one.'

'And that one,' added ffinch-Percy.

20

Piyumi woke up well past noon. Her first working weekend, so to speak! She luxuriated another half hour in bed. There was absolutely nothing planned for the day, nothing on her social calendar, except Marek who had promised to come round. She didn't feel the need to get up and make herself respectable for him, there was nothing he hadn't seen before.

Then she remembered the call. How could she have forgotten? She had been planning it all week. Her last chance. She dressed and crept into the main house praying nobody would be around.

Mr Skanda picked up on the first ring. 'You're lucky to catch me here today. You missed the last two Wednesdays.'

'I'm sorry,' she said. There had been too much happening in her own life lately to bother about anything else.

'I've tried you several times. Some woman keeps saying you're not in. Gedera na, gedera na.'

'Mr Skanda, would you be interested in buying this house?' she asked plunging straight in. 'All except for a small piece at the back which I want to keep. Half an acre in the best part of

Cinnamon Gardens, prime blue-chip real estate, an 8000-square-foot colonial mansion . . .' She could hear herself, breathless, like an overeager estate agent.

Calm down, she told herself, calm down! You don't want to sound too desperate.

'Yes.'

'What's that? I couldn't hear you.'

'Yes,' he replied again in his ponderous voice. 'I would have to ask my superiors, but I think I can say with fair certainty the answer will be yes.'

Piyumi sat down heavily on the hall chair. Had she heard right? Was this finally the end of all her troubles?

Could you say that again? she wanted to ask, but was very afraid the yes might turn into a no. She put the phone down. She looked at her legs which were shaking uncontrollably. She brought them up to her chin and put her arms around, hugging them to herself.

The minister was not in the habit of visiting prospective bridegrooms for his daughter. Matrimonial business was woman business. Or more specifically, Wife business. But he tacitly approved. Poopie was nineteen and eminently marriageable. In fact, in a year or two she would be over the hill. Already she had taken to wearing short skirts and hanging out in nightclubs. How often had he remonstrated with Evangeline about this sort of thing! But what could you expect from a woman who herself constantly refused to wear a sari to his political tamashas?

Poopie was at that dangerous time of life. If she wasn't fixed up very soon, if they let it go another year or two, there was a very real chance she might do something rash. Heavens, she might grow a moustache and join a foreign NGO! Originally, he had been all for a great political dynastic marriage, the daughter of the Honourable Minister of This marrying the son of the Honourable Minister of That. But a little reflection brought home to him how unnecessary this was. As minister, he knew he was destined for great things: the only way left to him was up: into the cabinet, the prime ministership and even beyond. If he fixed his daughter with someone already up there, people would say afterwards that that was the only reason for his own rise. (People were wicked, he knew that.) The marriage would steal much of his own political thunder.

He and Evangeline had next considered marrying Poopie off for money. But he already had oodles of the stuff, he didn't need any more. Sri Lankan society was very unforgiving and intransigent about things like that. Take his own case: however high he rose in politics, however successful he was in bringing prosperity to his country and honour to his people, he would always be known as that timber mudalali who cut down every tree from Dondra Head to Point Pedro for the money. Another mudalali in the family would be a fate worse than death.

Evangeline, of course, had been keen on fixing Poopie up with her very grand relations up at the Walauwa in Kandy.

Impecunious and hysterical, they had bloodlines as long as your arm. He remembered the treatment he had received from them in his day and he wasn't about to go through all that again. He had relied on them for their connections then. But he was minister now, and Evangeline could go stuff all their bloodlines up her skinny lurex bottom. Let them come to him now when they wanted jobs for themselves and places in good schools for their children. Let them beg.

So what do you do when you can marry your daughter off to virtually anyone in the country, but for reasons of your own don't want to? Simple. You play the foreign card. A foreigner, poor or rich, workman or aristocrat, had this one supreme advantage: he could not be classified neatly in any of the thousand and one drawers of Sri Lankan feudalism. He might speak the Queen's English, he might speak Cockney; he might not speak at all, having had his vocal chords surgically removed at the age of nine. It wouldn't matter. Rent-a-crowd would henceforth refer to him as that foreign husband of Poopie's. He could not be judged. That great blessing of colour-blindness between the races would be upon him.

Enter Marek, stage left, pursued by matrimonial matrons.

In the meantime, the minister had more pressing affairs to deal with. There was less than a fortnight to go till elections. The number of violent incidents was increasing and as usual each side was blaming the other. Then there were the totally unrelated incidents, personal vendettas, insurance scams: everything was laid at his door. The other day a fireworks factory in Pettah had gone up in flames. Who knew the real cause? Maybe the owners were crackers, maybe they were just having a blast. But of course he, the minister, got the blame.

In a week he was giving his big speech at the stadium. Today was the ideal day to work on it with Evangeline and Poopie out of the way. The atmosphere was conducive to deep and penetrative thought. He had called in his three most trusted interns to help. It was easier to work in the bedroom, of course it was. The other staff had strict orders not to disturb . . .

Evangeline and Poopie set off in the ministerial Jag. 'How do I look?' asked Evangeline anxiously, dabbing at her glowing upper lip with a tissue. Anyone would have thought she was the prospective bride. Poopie reclined on the grey leather seats luxuriously. It had been going on for at least a year, this business. A whole succession of spotty callow youths with premature beer bellies and an unfortunate excess of nasal hair. This one was meant to be different, a foreigner. As if that mattered. All men looked grey in the dark. She was already bored. Sublimely, exquisitely bored.

Yeah, yeah, yeah, she thought. Whatever.

From the top bedroom of the chummery, Princy and Percy watched the whole caravanserai go past, outriders and all. Princy noticed the grey Jag.

'Bitch,' he said to himself. 'Double bitch!'

With great difficulty Mrs Herath cajoled Marek out of his

sarong and into a pair of baggy cords. He was adamant about the rubber slippers though. He couldn't understand why shoes were so necessary to meet his landlady's sister. Anyone would think he was going on a blind date!

'Although Evangeline hasn't had the benefit of a decent life in England,' Mrs Herath was saying, 'my sister is very proper.'

She looked pointedly at Marek's feet. He was twirling the slipper round and round his big toe quite skilfully. There seemed to be quite an art to it. A sudden commotion and the party in the sitting room looked up to see Evangeline framed in the doorway. She was in a leopard print today, diaphanous and halter-necked, through which Marek could see . . . no, he really didn't want to see. He shut his eyes determinedly and thought of the first tragic thing that came into his head, the Central Bank bombing, exchange control, the free-floating rupee. Free-floating did you say? Aaargh . . .!

Evangeline was talking. '. . . she was at a loose end so I forced her to come along. We call her Poopie at home—in Sri Lanka we don't like to refer to family members by their real names—in fact her name is . . .'

Marek opened his eyes and promptly closed them again. Strange. There was a girl in front of him who looked just like Iresha.

'Mummy,' he heard her say in horrified tones. 'How could you! He's my teacher!' She turned and ran out of the room.

All those months of fit-and-fold had not been for nothing. Evangeline's reaction time was sharpened to a pinpoint.

'Quick!' she said to the security. 'After her!'

And so it happened that on that sleepy Sunday, the

inhabitants of Deal Place were treated to the sight of a distraught teenager in a short black dress running down the road followed closely by bodyguards, outriders, a cook and a wall-eyed waiter. They all disappeared into the garden of the chummery at the bottom of the road, and in so doing granted Princy and Percy their dearest wish.

That one, that one and that one!

It took quite a while for the runaway bride, the caterers and guests to be recalled; less two or three security guards who had unaccountably vanished into the bowels of the chummery. The party reconvened.

Evangeline bounced back into action, so to speak. Sitting next to Marek she had a sudden flash of recognition.

'I know who you are! You're the foreigner who comes to that crazy house three doors away!' She looked at him coyly. 'I see you without your shirt on.'

'I almost see you without yours,' he wanted to reply. She edged a little closer. (It was a two-seater sofa, there wasn't much to edge.)

'Now that we know who you are—in fact my daughter has spoken so often about you!—I am even more in favour of this match. And I know I speak for Ranjith too.'

'Mrs Rodrigo,' said Marek firmly, 'I am her teacher.'

Was this woman so thick? Couldn't she understand the ethics of the thing?

'You won't always be her teacher,' murmured Evangeline. She said it with such certainty Marek was tempted to wonder whether she had the gift of prophecy. 'Ranjith has so many businesses. He could easily fit you in.' The chiffon of her blouse hung uncomfortably close, a small spotted animal with a life of its own.

Marek got up sharply. 'I'll get you a drink.' Directing the wall-eyed waiter towards her, he fled outside into the garden.

Iresha was standing near the gate smoking. 'Cigarettes can kill you,' he said.

'If the embarrassment doesn't kill me first. I'm so sorry about this, sir. You must think my family are a bunch of morons.'

'You don't have to call me 'sir'. We're not at school now.'

'The funny thing is, I really, really like you.' She looked up at him with sudden hope.

What lustrous eyes, he thought, what a beautiful face! Unhappiness has yet to line it. It has a long way to go. Then he remembered his own unhappiness, a tiny seed buried deep in the small of his back.

'There is someone else,' he said.

21

Putting the phone down after her conversation with Mr Skanda, Piyumi looked around. Suddenly all the inanimate objects in the room seemed to her to throb with an energy of their own, glowing as if they were radioactive. This is how a terminal patient must feel, she thought, when they're suddenly told the case has been misdiagnosed, that there is no cancer after all.

Piyumi got up and stretched her arms. She did an experimental pirouette. She took the picture of Aunty Chelvam and the Pope off the grand piano and waltzed around with it for a bit.

'Mine!' she said dramatically, 'All mine!' and let off an evil stage laugh. She noticed Suranganee watching her quietly from the shadows.

'What are you doing?' Suranganee asked.

She blew her a kiss and waltzed off to the dining room from where there were sounds of clattering crockery and cutlery.

'Stop the sale!' she said.

They were all at lunch. 'What do you mean?'

She hugged the Pope to her breast. 'I'm buying it. I'm buying Serendipity.' At that moment she was so full of the milk of human kindness, she could have swept Aunty Pushpam off her feet and whirled her round the room. She could have sat with Dhanu and listened for hours to his Tales of LaToya.

'I have found a buyer.'

'Who?'

'You don't know him,' she said vaguely. 'Man called Skanda.'

'Skanda? We don't know any Skanda.'

She almost said, I don't know him either. Wisely, she refrained.

'He can deal directly with Sinnetambe,' said Bala. 'He'll have to match or better Nizam's offer.'

It occurred to her then that they were not quite as happy for her as she had imagined they'd be.

'And make sure,' said Ganga, 'that he's above board. There are lots of nefarious elements trying to get their hands on Colombo Seven property these days.'

'Nefarious? What a charming word,' she replied. 'I'm one hundred per cent sure he's nefarious.' She struck a Bharata Natyam pose. 'Well he's got to be, hasn't he, with a name like that?'

But Ganga was not amused. Piyumi could see the lines tighten around her mouth. 'Let me recite a little poem,' Ganga said. 'It might help you to put things in perspective.

'There was a young lady from Niger, Who smiled as she rode on a tiger, They returned from the ride, With the lady inside, And the smile on the face of the tiger.'

'Do I make myself clear?'

'Oh, Aunty Ganga,' said Piyumi sweetly, 'You're such a good poet, And you don't even know it!'

She waltzed out of the room with the Pope. Back in the pavilion on her own she wasn't so sure of herself. Her stomach was rumbling. (She could hardly go back in there and ask for food after such a brilliant exit line, could she?) Am I in the middle of some Faustian pact, some deal with the Devil? she asked herself, bouncing up and down on the rusty iron springs. Am I? Am I? Am I?

The next day, she went straight upstairs to Bilious, to see Sinnetambe.

'I have a buyer for Serendipity. His name is Skanda. Lives in London, at 8, Tremadoc Road, SW4.'

Sinnetambe stared at her.

'Can I ask him to get in touch with you?' Sinnetambe seemed to be searching his mind for something to say.

'Mr Sinnetambe, if you have anything to say, say it. I'm a big girl, I can handle it.'

What's wrong with these people! she thought angrily. They have the capacity to make even the simplest things complicated!

'Tell him to make his offer in writing,' Mr Sinnetambe finally said.

She got up. 'I'll do that. I'm sure he'll better Nizam's offer.'

Downstairs, she explained the circumstances to the girls at Women in Want.

'I have this buyer. The only one who'll let me keep the back bit for myself. I don't exactly know what his motives are, but I have a fairly good idea. So. Am I some sort of double-dealing, duplicitous bitch? Am I selling my principles downriver to gain for myself the only thing I ever seriously wanted in my life? And if so, is it worth it?'

'No!' said Cassie. 'Don't do it. Don't you know the meaning of the word integrity?'

'If integrity means being true to yourself, how do you know I'm not being true to myself?'

'Honey, you just go ahead and do what you have to do,' said Sharmila. 'If it's a question of sacrificing your principles to save your loved one, hell, I'd do it! And Serendipity does seem to be the love of your life.'

'This word integrity,' said Janaki. 'Do you know, it doesn't even exist in Sinhala or Tamil? I don't think anyone here understands the concept. What they do understand is expediency. Politicians happily jump into bed with the murderers of their kith and kin for the sake of expediency. I once sat next to a known murderer,' she said, her eyes going dreamy with the recollection. 'He introduced himself to me over the soup. He was the MP of somewhere or other. He'd pulled out a gun at a roadblock and shot a rival politician in cold blood. I could hardly eat anything that night. I was so pleased, it did wonders for my waistline.'

'So what you're saying is: it's wrong, but do it anyway, because it's what everyone else does.' Piyumi looked at them glumly. 'Fat lot of good you lot are.'

Whatever changed their minds about Mr Skanda was anyone's guess—perhaps Sinnetambe had called during the course of the day—but Piyumi came back to find the inhabitants of Serendipity galvanized into action by the thought of this mysterious buyer from London. Mr Nizam was one thing (Nizam's a good chap, he'll wait a month or two after handing over the money. This is Sri Lanka—how can we shift the belongings of four generations overnight?) but Mr Skanda quite another. The idea of him seemed to drive chill winds into the vacant spaces of their minds. He was from Abroad, he was For Real. You couldn't afford to mess with him.

The Art Deco Chinese carpets were all rolled up. Ganga was going through the silver cupboard, removing handles from entrée dishes, stacking them one inside the other. Everything was to go to the family coconut plantation up the coast beyond the airport. The fact that the plantation bungalow was a small cottage the size of Serendipity's back kitchen had only vaguely occurred to the Segarajasinghams.

They began to play a sort of Victorian parlour game called Will It Fit?

'Do you think we could hang the murano glass chandeliers from the cottage ceilings?'

'Of course.'

(The chandeliers were enormous, Aunty Chelvam's last profligate fling in Italy after that heady half-hour with the Pope. The Serendipity ceilings were fifteen foot high, the cottage's a mere eight. You'd have to be four foot nothing to avoid having your head knocked off by those heavy lead crystal droplets. It would be death by cut glass for anyone but a dwarf.)

There were coromandel screens and brass spittoons and elephant's foot umbrella stands. There were Imari tea sets and lacquered bamboo whatnots.

'Everything will be packed and stored at the cottage,' said Ganga firmly.

'And we'll all have to sleep outside under coconut trees because there's no room indoors,' muttered Bala. 'And when we get hit by falling coconuts it won't matter to her, she's soft in the head already.'

It was not clear whether Mr Skanda would be building apartments. Piyumi realized that the others didn't care one way or the other. There were plenty of apartment blocks springing up all over Cinnamon Gardens that they could move to. To them a flat was no different from a hot air balloon tethered to some vague spot on the ground: it didn't particularly have to be on the grounds of Serendipity. And for the hundredth time she thought, why am I so different? Why is even the air above Serendipity more special to me than the air above anywhere else? I have not lived here long enough to tell the difference. Is this just the fanciful zeal of the convert?

When Viraj drove her home that evening they promptly commandeered his services. In no time at all he was taking down pictures, packing books into boxes, dismantling almirahs. He had never seen so many beautiful things in his life. To cap it all, the girl in the pink dress was working by his side. He didn't dare look her directly in the face, but covertly inspected the downy hair on her arm, silently breathing in the faint aroma of Sunlight soap her skin exuded. The pearls of sarcasm falling from her lips were jewels beyond price.

Piyumi viewed all this activity with barely disguised satisfaction. The rest of them had a long way to go to their final destination up the coast. Her work was done, she had already arrived, she was installed: in her very own pavilion.

Viraj drove Marek to work early in the morning. From the Mogambo he cut across to Serendipity where he waited till Piyumi was ready. If he was lucky he could engage in a bout of verbal fisticuffs with Suranganee (he knew her name now, saucy little bitch). She always managed to get him worked up and once she'd fired her parting shot, she disappeared into the bowels of the big house, reappearing only at the end to close the gates as they left. By then it was usually too late for him to answer back. The moment was lost.

But Viraj was a worried man. Ever since the day of the white van incident, Lenin Marx Siddhu had been missing from the watte. There was nobody to pay the 250-rupee stipend he had got so used to receiving, the daily payment on the three-wheeler. Of course the foreigners he had been assigned to take care of, Piyumi and Marek, more than made up with their generosity. And this latest job helping out at the big house was an absolute windfall.

There was actually one person in the watte who did know where Lenin Marx Siddhu was. That was Celestina from the next lane. She knew that Lenin Marx had fled to Badulla to take refuge with his sister in the mountains till the white vans stopped cruising round. Celestina had the key to his small house: nobody else knew, it was a private arrangement.

Her friendship with Lenin Marx went back a long way. He had been one of her first clients in those glorious early days when she had first arrived at the watte, those days when she still had a waist. Her Tuesday night special he was, all the tricks, 500 rupees flat. Then one day he brandished a 1000-rupee note at her and she said, quite inexplicably,

'I don't have change. Pay me next time.'

She had plenty of change, hidden under her sarees in the steel almirah and no doubt he knew that. From then on neither raised the delicate matter of money. But the Tuesday night specials continued. It was a fair deal if you stopped to think about it. In exchange for love he gave her communism, shagging her like Che Guevara, pressing her up against the kitchen table with the urgency of his Marxist propositions. Together they shared the golden showers of her socialism, delighted in the dutiful doing of dogmas doggie-style.

It was difficult to say who was missing the Tuesday nights more. For Celestina it was business, business, business all the time now. Strange how the exchange of money took the pleasure out of things. I need a bit of light relief, she thought. Maybe I'll invite that young lad Viraj in for a cup of tea next time. After that foreign fiasco, it looks like he could do with a bit of R&R, poor little pet.

22

The party had been a disaster, even Mrs Herath had to admit that. Adding insult to injury the caterers had packed up all the remaining food—oh, there had been lots!—and taken it away under the instructions of Mrs Rodrigo to feed the ministerial security.

'Well that was a fine mess, that was,' said Mr Herath jovially.

'Oh, shut up,' said Mrs Herath with some asperity. 'You're getting parippu for dinner. That's all there is in the house.'

They had hardly seen the proposed bridegroom. He had locked himself up in his room straight after the festivities and disappeared to work early next morning. And no sooner had he gone than the final insult: the postman delivered a letter. Not a postcard for all the world to read but a proper letter, covered and sealed. With a Spanish stamp.

Mrs Herath could have steamed it over the kettle—it was the easiest thing in the world—and it was almost her duty to do so, the well-being of any lodger being of almost paramount importance to her in her capacity as landlady. But yesterday something inside had died, as that woman sang in the song. The stuffing had been knocked out of her, every moral fibre of her being vacuumed out. Why do I bother? she thought hopelessly.

At times like these she longed for her past life in London, in that vast council block in Stockwell (the common concrete stairway garnished generously with dog turds, the playground sowed every season with broken glass) and within the flat just she and Janaka: against the vast world they called London outside, clicking and whirring like a Heath Robinson machine.

When Marek arrived, he found the letter propped up against the telephone like a reproach. The Heraths were nowhere to be seen. He crept into his room.

The Palace of the Alhambra, it said at the top, The Gardens of the Generalife, Granada. He read the postcard:

'I had removed my shoes because my feet were beginning to kill me. Walk walk walk that's all we do and why do they build castles on top of hills I'd like to know. Dennis says I'm fussy but I'm not really. Anyway I'm bathing my feet in this ice cold stream when Dennis drops down. Look here says I, this is no time for nookie, there's people watching and you know what? Marry me he says, marry me. You could have knocked me down with a feather except I was down already. All right I say all right you don't have to act crazy about it but there and then he springs up and does this little dance. Mauritians are crazy though us Poles are crazier aren't we. Well there you are. I thought you'd like to know. Don't bother calling we're not there. (Don't call us we'll call you ha ha) We have Seville to do and Cordoba and God knows where. Dennis is a little Hitler when it comes to sightseeing, Ma.'

Marek folded the letter. He was putting it back in the envelope when he noticed a scrawl at the bottom.

'PS Dennis says I'm to move in downstairs with him. That lovely man Skanda has made me an offer on mine I can't refuse ha ha so there you are. Don't worry you know it's all money in the bank for you.'

'I have good news and bad news,' said Debs, popping out of her cubicle. 'The good news is that I am taking you on a field trip.' She beamed at Piyumi. 'The bad news? The bad news is that I'm afraid we can't share a room.'

There is a God after all, thought Piyumi. Outwardly she put on a suitably chastened look.

'It'll be hard, I know,' said Debs. 'But I need my sleep when we go outstation.' She patted Piyumi on the head. 'I hope you won't hold it against me.'

(How can I, Piyumi nearly asked, if we're in separate rooms?)

They would stay overnight in Giritale checking up on conditions of women in the small chena cultivations up there.

'Those wretched women!' Debs exclaimed. 'When you think of the succour I can give them!'

'Just imagine!' said Piyumi.

'It seems only I am there for them.'

'Poor women!' agreed Piyumi.

The girls gathered round after Debs had retired to her cubicle, congratulating her on her good fortune.

'I remember she took me to Giritale when I was first hired,' said Cassie dreamily. 'She taught me everything I know.'

'And you still know nothing,' snorted Sharmila. Piyumi wanted to tell them that in her case the teaching had been done a while back. She kept quiet.

Debs popped her head back out. 'Will you tell the three-wheeler driver we'll be needing his services? I'll be hiring a van of course. He can drive us.'

'Viraj,' said Piyumi. 'That's his name.'

At lunchtime she went to root Viraj out of the kade where he had taken to spending the mornings waiting for hires. He and the kade owner were best of friends. She joined them for a cup of coffee, hot and sweet and strong, three inches of grounds topped by half an inch of liquid.

'Mr Gunasiri and I are talking politics,' he grinned. 'So far we haven't been able to see eye-to-eye on a single thing!'

The elections were genuinely too close to call. Up and down the countryside, in kades like this, in churches, mosques and temples, people were arguing. Everyone had theories. Everyone had details of the latest conspiracy, the latest outrage. Sadly, nobody ever got it completely right.

After every assassination there was an inquiry which fizzled away to nothing in a few months. So you soon learnt not to expect results, not to have any memory lasting longer than five minutes. When outsiders said you were desensitized by war to the effects of violence, they were wrong: you were only turning the kaleidoscope another quarter turn in your hurry to get to another pattern, one that hopefully formed a prettier picture. There was no point lingering over incidents that had no resolution, designs that had no symmetry.

It was a tough call to make. On the one hand the minister felt he owed it to Poopie to be present at the Mogambo fundraiser. On the other hand what if there was press?

All government officials had to believe in the sanctity of the state school system. What they did in private was their own business but in public, officially, international schools were the Enemy. On the other hand there would be 800 voters in there, as good an election meet as any.

Matters were somewhat complicated by the knowledge that the leader of the opposition might be there too since his daughter was also a pupil. In the run-up to elections there was a tacit understanding that opposing parties would never appear on the same platform at the same time.

As it happened, at the last minute the opposition leader was invited to be chief guest at the Association of Left-Handers, at their annual jamboree the same night.

The minister was relieved—he wouldn't have to let his daughter down yet again—but also miffed. There were many more left-handers in the country than there were international school parents. (In fact in one famous election, all left-handers up and down the coast had abstained from voting and the results had actually swung the other way!) So why wasn't he asked to be the chief guest?

The interns took umbrage on his behalf.

'Left-handedness?' asked the first intern, outraged. 'What does the leader of the opposition know about left-handedness?'

'They say he is left-handed,' whispered the second intern.

'But our boss is ambidextrous!'

'You know that,' said the first intern winking. 'I know that. But the general public doesn't!' He nudged the other in the ribs.

Imbulgoda, Kadawatha, Pasyala—the suburbs squeezed out of the rear end of the van like toothpaste out of a tube. Viraj drove like a true three-wheeler kariar, cutting through the middle of village markets, bus queues, election rallies. No gap was too small to sneak through, no vehicle too fast to overtake; and all the while that rocking motion—accelerator, brake, accelerator, brake—like the cantering of a mechanized horse.

'I think,' said Debs faintly after about the tenth squeeze-through, the tenth near-death, 'I'll sit at the back if you don't mind.'

So Piyumi found herself in the hot seat next to Viraj. He turned round, looked at her and smiled, but all Piyumi could see was the gigantic articulated lorry ahead, bearing down on them with the unwelcome familiarity of a maiden aunt at a wedding. Viraj turned his attention back to the road just in time. There were various medals of the Madonna, Jesus Christ, the Lord Buddha and assorted Hindu gods dangling from the mirror. Piyumi tried praying to them individually, jointly and severally.

On and on they went.

'How about breakfast?' Debs asked weakly. Too late, they had already shot past the cool spot at Ambepussa. They turned off towards Dambulla and the road became wider, emptier. The electrical canter turned into a gallop, and soon—Piyumi had no doubt about it though her eyes were closed—they were airborne.

Like a concert pianist so technically accomplished he can afford to lose himself in the emotions of his music, Viraj drove by intuition rather than mere mechanics. Skirting a man-made lake, they shot up a hill, past an outraged security guard who tried unsuccessfully to stop them by bringing his bamboo barrier crashing down—too late! —and screeched to a halt in the forecourt of the Giritale Hotel.

Viraj massaged his neck mournfully. 'My reaction time,' he said. 'Just not what it used to be.'

The receptionist looked doubtfully at the three of them. 'I have two singles marked down here. Which of you is the double?'

But between car park and reception, Debs had rallied remarkably. Or maybe it was the dry zone air. 'We're Women in Want,' she boomed. 'He'll be in the drivers' quarters.'

Below them, the lake, the scrub jungle, the rolling hills all lay silver-edged and bleached of colour, every bit as unreal as one of those landscapes in a Victorian water-colourist's mind.

'The Rajarata,' he said proudly. 'Land of the Ancient Sinhala Kings.'

'The ancient Sinhala and Tamil kings,' Piyumi corrected him gently.

Debs had left them and joined three men at the next table. They were playing cards and passing round a bottle of arrack. Every now and then there was a spectacular burp and they all guffawed loudly.

'Those ancient kings were far more cosmopolitan than we give them credit for. There were plenty of instances of Tamil generals faithfully serving Sinhala kings, and vice versa.' She looked round. 'And of course the last kings of Kandy were Tamil.'

'They were bad people,' he said. 'Do you know, one of them made a woman pound the head of her child in a mortar? That's why we had to get rid of them.'

'The penalties for treason were just as barbaric in England a hundred years before that,' she said earnestly. 'You can't judge one civilization by the standards of another, particularly if they're at different stages of development.'

But she could see she was losing him. He had better things to worry about than history: the school books for his sister's child, the medicines for his grandmother. So she tried a different tack.

'Who decided that that mad king of England, George III, was better for us Sri Lankans than our own king, however barbaric he might have been?'

'The nobles decided,' said Viraj confidently. 'Our leaders.'

'And you're sure they only had the people's best interests

at heart? That they weren't doing this for power or greed or any of a thousand other reasons? Are you sure they were so very different from our leaders of today?'

He was silent.

'Did you know,' she said, 'that the British kings for the last 300 years have been German? That till fifty years ago, they spoke only German among themselves? How could that be any different from a Sri Lankan king in Kandy speaking Tamil?'

She had lost him entirely. The very fierceness of her argument, the heat of her rhetoric had driven him to take cover in the shadows. You have to be gentle, she reprimanded herself. You can't win anybody's mind by force. But still she couldn't help letting her feelings get the better of her.

'Look at me,' she said almost tearfully. 'My mother's Sinhalese, my father's Tamil. Who decides for me what I should be? Why can't I be both, and be Sri Lankan, and be proud of it?'

But he didn't have to say anything. The unspoken emotions of war lay all about them, flying quietly below the clouds of their subconscious like planes below the radar: You're either with us or against us. You decide.

He walked her back to her room and in the corridor, in the dark, she found somehow he had taken hold of her hand. She unlocked the door and gently pulled him in, noting as she did the flicker of worry on his face that Debs was just next door.

What's wrong with me, she thought almost joyously, that I should be bedding just about every character in this book? And in a flash the answer came back to her, floating like a little golden duck on the bath of her happiness: If I were a man

I shouldn't be agonizing over this, I'd just be happy to go with the flow.

Halfway through the night she heard Debs blundering about next door, crashing into things and cursing. There was silence for a bit and then the snoring began, loud as a CTB bus at the Dehiwala flyover. The beds lay headboard to headboard, separated by the thinnest of partitions, and it was almost as if Debs were in the bed with them, the genial ghost of their lovers past.

Through a chink in the curtain she saw the moonlight in the sky reflected off the lake.

Next day they began the visits from hut to hut, from one small patch of cultivation to the next. Everywhere they could smell the sharp acrid odour of the jungle, feel the heat from the clear skies pressing down upon them like a blanket of thorns.

From a black sack she carried around, Debs doled out a packet of milk powder and a packet of biscuits to every household. These were on her own account, not paid for by any NGO.

'Nobody told me they were allowing suddhas into parliament now,' said one enthusiastic small-holder. 'This foreign gentleman shall certainly get my vote.'

23

'Friends!' said Percy ffinch-Percy. 'Today at Equal Ground we stand proud of the power of the pink rupee!' He looked down at his papers. 'Oops! Wrong speech. Let me start again. Honourable Minister, Honourable Governor, ladies and gentlemen, welcome to the Mogambo Fund-raiser . . .'

The bodyguards, who had perked up at the mention of the pink rupee, went back to sleep again behind their dark glasses.

The Heraths, the minister and Mrs Rodrigo had made a spectacular last-minute entrance, elbowing their way to the front with a maximum of fuss and a minimum of discretion. She was wearing a poncho in violently multi-coloured stripes, and what looked like a large Mexican sombrero. (The result of two glorious weeks at that casino in Cancún where the ministerial party had checked in to investigate the deleterious effects of gambling on the common man.) She looked, unfortunately, like a singing waiter lost on the way to the Mexican evening at Cinnamon Grand. Establishing herself comfortably in the front row, she effectively blocked the view of the row behind, occupied by Mrs Fernando (the long-suffering wife of ICT Fernando) and two charming Fernandolings. Every time Evangeline looked to the right, the Fernandos plunged desperately to the left. They had just settled into this position when she turned again, leaving them to plunge desperately in the other direction. Mrs Fernando and her brood had wandered into these seats by mistake (the staff were supposed to be in free seating up in the balcony) and nobody had the heart to throw her out so there was a sort of rough justice to the whole thing.

The two sisters, Evangeline and Dulcie, chatted all the way through the first item.

'Where's you-know-who, dear?'

'Who dear?'

'You know . . . Poopie's friend.'

'I don't know, dear.'

They scanned the audience (the Fernandos plunging furiously from side to side) but there was no sign of Marek. In fact, he had taken one look at them and fled backstage.

'And who is that?' asked Evangeline. 'He looks like a bit of all right to me.'

'Don't get too excited dear. He's only a three-wheeler kariar,' said Mrs Herath. She looked carefully. 'Don't look now, but he's sitting with that odd girl, the friend of you-know-who.'

'Who dear?'

'You know . . . Poopie's friend.'

Getting hopelessly confused, they lapsed into silence. 'You'll have to take me to meet your parents, your grandmother,' Piyumi was saying.

Viraj squeezed her hand and said nothing. Why not just enjoy the moment? Why go and spoil it all?

Further on in the front row was the Governor, with for once, a surprisingly silent mobile. He was not interested in fund-raisers, only funds. In fact, this sort of thing usually sent him to sleep. He closed his eyes luxuriously and began counting Pajeros the way other people might count sheep. (One Pajero, two Pajero, three Pajero, four. Five Pajero, six Pajero, seven Pajero, more.)

Next to him Somawathie, daughter of the opposition leader, viewed the crowd with some satisfaction. The number of women with jewelled pins in their hair had increased dramatically. In fact, the whole ethnic thing was quite marked, a vindication of her stance on the matter. Unfortunately, that evening she herself was in uniform: a little black dress, little black fingernails.

At that moment a woman in a curry-yellow ball gown began shrieking plaintively onstage and Evangeline pulled her sombrero down firmly over her ears. When she hit top F she accidentally set off the Governor's mobile, momentarily waking him up.

'See sharp or you'll be flat!' said Mr Herath jovially, to no one in particular.

At the interval there was the press in the form of Maleeshya of *Chi!! Magazine* ('Oh, God,' said the minister), Evangeline moving this way and that for the cameras, the Fernandos plunging in counterpoint behind her like some sort of unpaid chorus line. And then the main event of the evening, the fashion show.

There were sarees of silk and sarees of cotton; sarees of jute which looked like gunny sacks and sarees of net which looked like bedroom curtains. (In fact they were bedroom curtains, hastily cut up and re-assembled by Raf and sewn with spangles.)

The models were even more assorted, unusually tall and big-boned, unusually lovely. There was one with cascading auburn hair and almond eyes that caught the eye of the minister. He turned to the burly bodyguard next to him.

'That one,' he said.

All too soon the evening came to an end and Percy was back onstage to roaring applause.

'And now all you village people, you complete gamayas, it's time to boogie your cares away, to the sounds of YMCA!' He looked down at his papers in alarm.

'Wrong again!' he said, stamping his foot petulantly.

The burly bodyguard forced his way backstage. 'There ought to be laws against people like you,' said Princy, peeling off his cascading auburn wig. 'But give me your number anyhow.'

She could hear the scratching and scrabbling long before she was fully awake. It sounded like a sort of large rat at the window shutters. Cautiously, she opened them a crack.

'Let me in,' he whispered. She could see the top of his silvery head, the pointy silvery beard. She unbarred the door and asked, 'Are you back now?'

He shook his head. 'Nobody must know I'm even alive, understand? I want you to do something for me.'

Celestina felt a frisson of excitement rippling through her nether regions.

'I want you to go to Pettah and get six yards of khaki PVC. They have specially wide rolls. It needs to be at least eight feet wide.'

'Ooh,' she squealed, 'is this for a new game we're going to play then?'

He gave her a pained look.

'Two men will bring a car here and park it in your front yard. Cover it with the PVC so it won't cause too much comment.'

She looked at him uncomprehendingly.

'I don't have enough room in my own yard. Besides it's being watched.'

'What'll I tell my customers?'

'Tell them,' he said thinking, 'tell them Viraj's foreign girl asked permission to park it here. It won't be for long.'

'And how long are you here for?'

'I have to leave for Badulla before dawn. Before I'm seen.'

'That's in an hour,' she said.

So they went inside and practised a little socialism for an hour.

Piyumi's cousin Dhanu was leaving. Of late, the calls from La Toya in Alabama had been increasing in frequency. 'I've used up my annual leave, my sick leave, my casual leave. I won't have a job to go back to if I don't go now.Nor a fiancée,' he added.

Piyumi was genuinely sorry to see him go. More sorry she hadn't used the time profitably to get to know him better. There had been more exciting things on her plate.

It occurred to her how different they were: America seemed to have washed him clean of any taint of the original sin of being Sri Lankan.

'I'm American first and last,' he said. 'Any Sri Lankan-ness is only a chilli flavouring sprinkled lightly on top.' And a generation on, she thought, even that won't be there. Oh yes, it might perhaps live on in the creaking curiosity of the name, much as there were Greek or Jewish or Armenian names in the New World: but in the main what you had to pass on to your children was the comforting blanket of your ignorance, the crushing certainty of your indifference to anything outside America itself.

Why am I so different? she thought. From whom have I inherited this long memory, these exquisite agonies of indecision? Maybe I am like this because they brought me from the ancient world to the old world: which has its own mildewed attics, its own quiet corners of corruption where spores float invisible in the air, continuing to reinfect me.

'Bala's driving me to the airport,' Dhanu said. 'Saturday evening. The flight leaves at six.'

'How will you sign the papers if you're not here?' she asked curiously.

'I've left my power of attorney with Aunty Pushpam.' He took her hand in a sudden gesture of affection. 'Come with us to the airport. Just come along for the drive!'

She shook her head. The morning after the Giritale trip Debs had come into the office with the magic words:

'I want you to write a report.' Afterwards, the girls surrounded her.

'Bitch!' they said pinching her good-naturedly. 'It's far too early in your career to be writing reports.'

Inwardly Piyumi glowed with the grace of this sacrament so unexpectedly bestowed. I must do a perfect job, she told herself. I mustn't let them down.

'I have a long report to write,' she told Bala and Dhanu reluctantly.

'So bring it along. I have to take a load of stuff to the cottage after dropping Dhanu. I was thinking of staying the night. Bring your report. We can make an evening of it.'

The night of the concert had been particularly fraught for Marek. He had been happily selling tickets with his friend Fernando from ICT when Mrs Fernando arrived, with two charming Fernandolets in tow.

'You!' she said. 'I want to talk to you.'

Having extracted him from behind the counter and the baleful influence of her husband she began to berate him.

'You're my husband's friend, you'd better talk to him.

I don't know what you've done to him but after he began associating with you he's turned into a raving heterosexual. By night and day! (Mrs Fernando's command of English was not what it might have been.)

'Me, I don't even get a look in now. Every day there are women (women!) at the door, demanding tuition from him, tuition in this, tuition in that. They pay for one hour and stay for three!

'At times,' she said bitterly, 'he's no better than a male prostate. Just this morning there was a girl who came at nine and stayed till twelve. You know what I did after she left? I burnt the cushion she was sitting on.'

Even now there was a whiff of smoke about her. Out of the corner of his eye Marek could see the ministerial party approaching. 'Madam,' he said desperately. 'Please go through, the concert's about to start. Sit anywhere you like.'

Marek then fled backstage to be confronted by the spectacle of Piyumi and Viraj in the front row, holding hands and canoodling throughout the show. It was more than a man could bear. She doesn't know what she wants, she's never had a steadying influence in her life. Those legs, he thought with an unexpected flash of crudeness, will open up to anything that comes between them. They've had more traffic recently than the A-9.

Added to that, there was not much room in the wings and Iresha kept brushing up against him. Her dress was even shorter than usual, her nails even blacker. As for the creaminess of those thighs . . . can I be in love with one woman and still be turned on by another? Marek asked himself hopelessly. It was a question he didn't have the answer to. Perhaps it was a question for Father Stanislaus at St. Mary's Clapham.

By the time the fat lady began to sing, his mind was made up. I don't care if she doesn't love me back, I'm going to ask her to marry me. I'll ask her outright. I'll force her to make up her mind.

24

It was the perfect weekend. The foreign visitors were gone, Mr Bala was gone. Suranganee was weeding the flowerbed furthest from the house, the one nearest the front gate. Every so often a cry emanated from one of the upper balconies.

'Suranganee!'

Then a more desperate, 'Suranganeeee!' Suranganee studiously ignored these. There were only women left in the house, Ganga, Pushpam and the cook. The women were on the whole more self-sufficient than the men. They were also more realistic. They called twice. When you didn't answer, they knew you weren't going to. So they got on with it. They didn't bother you again.

'When in doubt, do without,' said Suranganee, mentally wagging a finger at them.

She turned her attention to the flowers. 'When in doubt pluck it out,' she said pulling up handfuls of green stuff. Weeding for her was therapeutic, cathartic. Nothing much flowered near the gates.

When the two men rang the bell she didn't have far to go.

Through the bars she assessed them for social status. They had none. They weren't fit for the front steps, let alone the front verandah.

'We've come for the car,' said one, jiggling a bunch of keys at her through the bars as if she were some sort of ape in the zoo. Jiggle, jiggle, jiggle.

Under normal circumstances she would have told them where to get off. But they had mentioned the magic word. The car was an affront to her every sense of decorum and dignity. It was unquestionably the biggest weed in her garden. In fact, if you thought about it, it was the social equivalent of those two outside the gates.

'You can have it,' she said, opening the gates wide. With all my heart, she might have added under her breath. It wasn't necessary to consult Ganga or Pushpam. She knew where they stood on the matter. The fact that Piyumi was away at the estate and couldn't object only lent a certain pleasure to the proceedings.

Marek arrived just as the car was leaving. 'Who's that?' he asked.

Suranganee shrugged eloquently. Sri Lankan staff are practised in the art of shrugging, and in this Suranganee was first among equals.

'Does Miss Piyumi know about this?'

Another shrug. Marek made as if to come in but she barred his way. As with all good staff who have a sixth sense about the private lives of those they work for, she instinctively knew his star was on the wane, that he had been replaced in Piyumi's affections by that nasty three-wheeler kariar.

Disgusting, yes, but there was no accounting for the tastes of these foreign women. To give up a suddha for that!

'Miss Piyumi gone,' said Suranganee. 'Estate.' She shrugged again. 'Coconuts,' she said jiggling a bit, somewhat surreally.

Mystified, Marek went away.

Two rather rundown brick pillars supported a low iron gate which was opened after a while by a surly local in a hil-hil vest and a sarong from the time of Sigiriya. His mouth remained open long after the gate had closed and the Toyota Crown driven through. The grey ghosts of coconut palms leant crazily in all directions, and everywhere the whispering of those shaggy heads telling tales of the latest happenings to each other in conspiratorial tones. The red laterite road wound on and on, crossed by endless alleys stretching as far as the eye could see, each as long as the nave of some great green Gothic cathedral, cross-vaulted and lit by dappled tropical light, and hung with bunches of coconuts.

'That's the block your mother sold,' said Bala, pointing to it, 'before she took you off to England. The best block. It faces the lake on the other side.'

There was an unspoken criticism there that Piyumi chose to ignore. After what seemed an interminable drive, they arrived at the cottage, two rooms separated by a small sitting area. A passion vine grew in profusion over the low roof and there were narrow verandahs at the front and back. 'This was only a cowshed that your great grandfather converted. After the Land Reform Commission took over most of the plantation. Naturally they wanted the best bit, the bit with the original estate bungalow.'

Piyumi looked up. She had never heard such bitterness in his voice before.

'So you see, in our time we've had to put up with more than mere terrorism. Before that there was envy and greed, thinly disguised as socialism. The original bungalow,' he said pointing through the trees, 'is now used as a place where local big-wigs bring their comfort women.'

He took her on a conducted tour, pointing out special shrubs cultivated for their nitrogen-fixing properties and their loppings—glyricidia and acacia and ipil-ipil—and the decorticator that turned these loppings into bite-sized bits; the gassifier that turned them into energy to run the estate generator. These were not features of your normal Sri Lankan coconut plantation. She realized with a shock that gentle mild-mannered Bala ran one of the most ruthlessly efficient and scientifically advanced estates on the island. No wonder he didn't care too much about Serendipity. This was what he saved his energies for!

And then, the pièce de résistance. He made her climb a narrow, almost vertical metal staircase to the concrete platform of a disused water tank which he had converted into a one-room dwelling.

'The Bird's Nest.' He grinned. 'This is where I'll be most of the time while the women fight it out back there in the cottage.'

There was a bed that swung gently on iron chains, a minute sink, a covered w.c. Below them a sea of woolly green heads bowing and twittering to each other good-naturedly. You couldn't see the ground.

'I'm happy here,' he sighed. 'I don't need anything back in Colombo. But you know women.' He poured them each an arrack and ginger beer.

'Go back,' he said quietly.

'I beg your pardon?'

'Go back. You're too innocent for this place.'

She began to argue but he raised a hand to silence her. 'Hear me out. You people in the diaspora, you've got used to a simpler way of life in the West, a life protected by society, by the state. Your rules are more clear-cut, the arrows of your justice fly straighter than ours. It's no good viewing our picture through your eyes: you'll see only the outlines of it, the cartoon of the painting if you like. It takes at least twenty years of living here for the true colours to emerge, for the picture to start making any sense.'

Piyumi said nothing, swirling the drink round and round in her glass.

'This is not to say our life is any worse than yours. On the contrary. The bespoke, hand-stitched quality of it . . . you'd be hard-pushed to find its equal anywhere in the world.'

'It makes me laugh,' he continued, 'when foreign dignitaries are helicoptered in for three hours and helicoptered back out. They return to London or New York and make meaningful statements, pronounce judgment. What a joke.'

'But I want to be here,' she said desperately. 'I want to

make a go of things. I realize it'll be different once I'm living here permanently.'

'Do you?' His voice was cold. 'Do you realize our lives here are built on a fragile eco-system of good manners and common decency that you outsiders are doing your best to erode, however well-intentioned you may be? Fifty years ago I could go out for a drink and come back late at night and only worry about getting copped for drunk driving. Today I can't even go out at night. It's not the drunk driving I worry about. It's the harassment I'll get from those same cops. So what's changed? Not the Sinhalese. It's our militancy that's upped the stakes, that's made both sides more intransigent.'

She didn't have the heart to argue. He was such a lovely man, the closest to her in that family.

'Go back before it's too late,' he said again quietly. 'You're in way over your head on this one.'

And that's the last thing I'll do, she thought. Silently she raised her glass to his and smiled.

They drove back late on Sunday night laden with farm produce: the small-leafed spinach that grew wild under the trees, the lemons large and coarse-skinned, the bunches of long green plantains. And of course, the week's supply of coconuts. The cook required one coconut per curry per day.

'We'll all die of heart attacks,' cried Pushpam.

'Rats!' said the cook. 'They can get somebody else if they want to economize. I can't cook with less.'

They were unloading stuff on the front verandah when the phone rang. Suranganee sprang to it.

'No,' she said, 'she's not here. I'm absolutely sure.' She looked round and started guiltily. Piyumi was standing right behind her. 'Oh, hold on a minute, I think she's just come in. Here you are.'

'Piyumi darling, at last! I've tried so often, you're never there!'

'No,' said Piyumi grimly, 'apparently not.'

Mrs Segarajasingham coughed delicately. 'It seems dear, you've been seen out and about quite a bit with, with a three-wheeler kariar.'

'Yes?'

'You know, dear, I wonder if it's quite the thing for people of our . . . people of our . . .'

'People of our what, mother?'

'Well you know, dear.'

'Viraj and I are very happy,' said Piyumi firmly. 'And yes, Mother, I am well, thank you so much for asking.'

'But darling, what are you going to do?'

'Learn to drive a three-wheeler of course,' said Piyumi crashing the phone down.

But she had forgotten that First Law of Serendipity: Never tell lies about the future, for they will become truths before your back is turned.

25

It was Viraj who noticed next morning that the car had gone.

'Where's the car?' Piyumi asked Suranganee. Suranganee shrugged, a shrug that was eloquence itself.

'They came to collect it.'

'Why did you let them take it away?' Suranganee shrugged again.

It was not that Piyumi minded one bit. She hardly used it these days anyway, preferring the three-wheeler for work. It was a vague disquieting feeling she had that things were moving beyond her control, that the train was pulling out of the station, the platform silently gliding past. She was no longer part of the bigger picture, whatever that was supposed to be.

'Let me make some enquiries,' Viraj said. He sounded rather mysterious.

The two sisters were on the phone to each other, Mrs Rodrigo opening the proceedings.

'And how are things with you-know-who, dear?'

'Not good, dear. Hardly speaks to me now. And Poopie?'

'Hardly speaks to me.'

'Tell her, dear. Tell her she could do a whole lot worse than marry a teacher. After all, you married Ranjith.'

'And you married Janaka . . . and look where that got you.'

There was a pause while the two sisters opened their hearts to these arrows. Then, having each successfully blooded the other, they settled in for a nice long gossip.

'Coming for tea?' the girls asked Piyumi at three o'clock that afternoon after Debs had left for her meeting.

Piyumi shook her head. 'I must get the first draft finished today.'

The girls retired to the cubicle at the back and Piyumi worked on. She found she couldn't read her notes on one of the households. Maybe Viraj will remember, she thought, let me go and ask.

It was that dead hour of afternoon and the streets were deserted, except for the odd person or two shimmering in the distance as if in a mirage. She saw Mr Gunasiri sitting moodily behind a glass cage of fly-blown sweetmeats but the kade was empty. So was the three-wheeler. Strange, she thought. The air was thick and soupy, enclosed and contained by the great overturned bowl of yellow sky. Far away she heard the dull metallic clang of temple bells as if someone was knocking to be let in.

Then she saw it, twenty yards in front of her, the white van, and wondered how she could have missed it. Two men were trying to close the back of it. Something was stuck in the doors. A leg. She recognized the white tracksuit bottom, the trainer. Without thinking, she ran, hurling herself against the closing doors. She began pulling at the leg oblivious to the men on either side. She felt a touch of cold steel at her temple. There was a click and she took strange comfort in that sound: it was like a full stop to what had always seemed the very long sentence of her life.

And then she heard herself scream. A raucous primal noise from deep down, from a place she didn't know she had. Whatever it was the men had been expecting, it wasn't that. They sprang into the van and began revving it up. She pulled again at the leg. The body landed with a bump on the road as the van sped away. She half dragged, half carried it back to the three-wheeler with a strength she didn't know she had.

'Mr Gunasiri!' she shouted. 'Did you get the number?'

Mr Gunasiri sat there impassively.

'Didn't you see the van?' she asked hysterically.

'What van?'

She looked round hopelessly. 'Watch over him while I go and get help! Please?'

But Mr Gunasiri sat motionless behind his cakes, making no move to come out of the shop. I can't leave him here unattended, she thought desperately, they might come back.

And so it was that the challenge she had thrown fate flew straight back in her face, and she had to teach herself how to drive a three-wheeler in all of five minutes. There were faint moans coming from the back as Viraj regained consciousness but she didn't dare stop. As she drove, careering wildly from side to side, it struck her how improbable was the chance of her actually being down there on that deserted street at that hour! She shivered.

The cop at the roadblock near Serendipity was well used to the behaviour of its strange inhabitant. He raised an eyebrow at the slumped figure in the back and waved her through.

With Suranganee's help she lifted Viraj onto the iron bed.

'Shouldn't we be taking him to hospital?' Suranganee asked.

Piyumi shook her head. There seemed to be nothing seriously wrong with him apart from a few cuts and scrapes. The effects of the chloroform were wearing off. How would you explain these events at a hospital? As so often happened, the accuser would become the accused. She thought of Bala's arrows of justice flying in curves not straight lines. Go back, he had said. You're in way over your head on this one.

As shadows lengthened on the lawn outside and the yellow sunlight deepened imperceptibly to gold and then bronze, she realized she was exhausted. She crawled into the bed with him. Cradling his head in her arms she looked down at his semi-conscious form. It was a body she had lately got to know well, the weight of it, the quantity of it; its hidden pathways; the strange treasures it yielded up under her patient persuasion.

Perhaps, she thought a little light-headedly, this is what serendipity has always had me down for: The Wayward Life of a Tuk-Tuk Wife.

In the early hours of the morning, he shook her awake. 'My parents will be worried,' he said.

'Go back to sleep,' she replied. 'It's still dark outside.'

When they did finally awake, it was mid-morning and Viraj's parents had gone to work. His elderly uncle was at home.

'I knew you'd be worried. I came to say I'm fine.'

'I can see you're fine,' said the old man irritably. 'You didn't have to come all this way to tell me. And who's this?'

'My girlfriend from England.'

'He's brought another girl,' the old man said in an aside to the TV. 'Says she's foreign. Looks Tamil to me.' Closer inspection revealed a minute, craggy, ancient woman next to the TV, sitting on an easy chair swinging her legs. Viraj's grandma.

'I preferred the other one,' said Grandma. 'More body to her.'

It was like being at the theatre when the spotlight moves away from the main action to highlight a separate group talking among themselves. The audience understands the theatrical convention that this is a different scene. Grandma and Uncle were definitely in a different scene.

'Hi there!' said Piyumi breaking in. 'I'm from London. My name's Piyumi Segarajasingham.'

'I told you,' said the old man to Grandma. 'Tamil.'

Afterwards Viraj took Piyumi through the watte. There were colonies like this all over Colombo—vast chunks of land packed dense with people—that didn't figure on any map, like Black Holes in a map of the universe. She saw the double row of latrines in the centre, the pot-bellied children bathing at pipes, the bits of gold and brown polythene buntings left over from the day of the rally. And in every house a TV as big as the front door. They turned down the cul-de-sac towards the cemetery.

Celestina was out hanging her laundry. 'Where's Lenin?' asked Viraj.

'Dead,' said Piyumi. 'In Moscow.'

'Nonsense!' snapped Celestina. 'He's alive. In Badulla.' She clapped a hand over her mouth realizing what she'd just said. 'At least that's what other people are saying.'

'What's he done with the car?'

Celestina thought a bit. 'That foreign girl!' she said brightly. 'Asked me whether she could park it here.'

'Did I now,' said Piyumi grimly.

There was definitely something in the water supply. These watte residents, they were all mad as hatters.

Viraj's fame spread far and wide with news of his escape. He was the local hero down at the gym. After all, it's not just anyone who gets to be hunted down by a white van, especially one equipped with a bolt gun. There was much discussion about this last piece of weaponry. A bolt gun to the temple is the humane method of stunning cattle before you kill them. So it is only the most merciful, the most compassionate of murderers who will use one on a human. It is also merciful towards the murderer in that it leaves behind no incriminating bullet; though naturally this was not the priority concern here.

Nobody stopped to think why they might have been hunting Viraj in the first place, Viraj least of all. The easy money (the wine, the women, the three-wheelers) was already a given in his young life; the ascent into adulthood and thuggery a natural part of growing up and being Sri Lankan. It was glamorous enough that he was being hunted at all: it added a credibility, a legitimacy to his life it might otherwise have lacked.

Deep down Piyumi had the sinking feeling it was somehow all to do with her. She tried not to think about it, hoping this feeling would go away. In the meantime she clung to him like clinging to a precious piece of salvage. She had saved his life! She was forever in his power.

Even though the rescue had brought them closer than ever, Viraj was loath to mention his new girlfriend, or her role as his saviour, to his friends. He couldn't understand his own reluctance: he was just acutely aware of it. There was a difference in age of about ten years between them.

'She's old!' his friends would have said. Debs had been even older but that was different. To be white was to be forgiven everything, even age. Piyumi had the supreme disadvantage of being the same skin colour as Viraj, and no amount of Britishness could wipe that out. She would have been mortified had she been aware of these very indigenous thought processes which Viraj kept to himself. In the meantime she was on the highest of highs. She had saved a lover, a house, a country. Well no, not a country. Not yet.

But Viraj would have been wise to keep in mind, too, that other little-known Law of Serendipity: Beware of those who save your life: understand that it will never be in your power to return the favour.

26

The entire upstairs rooms of Fuk-a-Luk Café were filled to overflowing with the opposition. It was the last week before the elections. The Sri Lankan cabinet was the largest in the world—a hundred and counting—so the shadow cabinet was even larger, on the principle that a man's shadow is always larger than he is.

'They'll win by a flood, a landslide!' said the shadow minister for natural disasters, always something of a disaster himself.

'By far the biggest disaster is agriculture,' said the leader. 'We need to improve cultivation, diversify crops. We mustn't be afraid to try new things.'

'Well, they're growing ganja in Moneragala.'

'My point entirely. Agriculture's really gone to pot.'

'Do you realize they've promised people a large port?'

'Personally,' sighed the shadow minister of ports, 'I'd prefer a large brandy. Lots of ice.'

'And that's another thing. They've decided to ban alcohol.'

'They can't do that! That's our idea!'

'So let's go one better, 'said the shadow minister for the upliftment of spirits. 'Let's ban liqueur chocolates. And maraschino cherries if you like.'

'What this country seriously lacks is energy,' continued the leader.

'I could hardly get up this morning, I was so tired,' yawned the shadow minister for the dawning of a new era (Five-Year Plan).

'. . . hydropower, coal, oil . . .'

'Must be this swine flu, I think.' The shadow minister for the dawning of a new era (Five-Year Plan) sneezed loudly.

'Cancel that order of spare ribs,' said the leader hastily to the hovering waiter. He rapped his glass with a knife for silence.

'Friends,' he said loudly. 'We are gathered here for the last time before the election. I don't want to alarm you, but their man Rodrigo has us all driven into a corner like pigs in a pen. It's time to break free, cure the country and save our bacon in the process.'

There were grunts and snorts of approval all round.

Marek had barely got over the letter from Granada when the next one arrived. It was postmarked London, and Mrs Herath treated it with all the vituperation it deserved.

'Well it's happened and I can't say I'm sorry. We just went him and me to that registry office off the King's Road. I did ask that lovely Mr Skanda from upstairs to come as witness He said yes and never turned up, typical! So we went to the office next door and rooted out two witnesses, a young Asian student who kept speaking to me in Welsh do I look Welsh I ask you and a cleaner called Mrs Mulhern. Dennis says he's going to treat me like a Queen from now on no more cleaning for me so I asked Mrs Mulhern could I hire her but she says she doesn't do south of the river more's the pity. So there you are its hello Mrs Ridoynauth goodbye Mrs Markovic ha ha I know you're far too busy with that new girl to want to come back but tell me when you do and I'll book you a nice B&B on Clapham Common. As for the new girl be careful, they're all after your money only its my money ha ha so you better be good to me or else, Ma.'

Marek knew the ground floor flat well. It had once had the best fireplaces, glossy black things of polished Welsh slate with shiny red and green Minton tiles. It also had access to a small patch of garden out the back with a quince tree. But only one bedroom.

He thought of all the love and care his father had lavished on that house over the years, and how he would never be able to sleep under its roof again. It was only one more sadness in a long line of sadnesses, and a comfort in its way because it was not entirely unexpected. They're sealing off my exits one by one, he thought. He had come to Sri Lanka purely on a whim, no pressure from anyone. At that time it had seemed to him there were plenty of other choices he might have made. Looking back, he realized with a shock there had actually only ever been the one.

The speech was finished and all were set to go. The house was emptying of interns. From her vantage point upstairs, Evangeline saw the last few staggering around the formal garden among the obelisks. They seemed to be having difficulty walking, obviously exhausted, the poor dears! Oh well, that's what you got when you worked directly under the boss.

Copies of the speech had been dispatched in advance to newspapers all over the world (from Honolulu to Rarotonga) so eager fans could imbibe its contents, sitting at their breakfast tables over boiled manioc and vitamin- enriched cassava juice. It was not a long speech. The essence of popularity, the minister had discovered long ago, was to keep it short (in private moments he wondered just how far he would have failed to go if he had been an inch or two taller). He fully expected this speech to jet propel him to hitherto unexplored places.

Evangeline was already dreaming of her own suite at Temple Trees, the prime ministerial residence on Galle Road, situated on that stretch of wasteland between Colpetty Junction and Galle Face Green. The area was littered with the debris of half-finished skyscrapers that looked more like coconut scrapers, rusty and expressionist, their mirrored glass tarnished, their concrete stained even before they were complete. (Oh, when would these award-winning architects learn that modernism didn't stand a chance against the elements when you built at the tropical seaside?)

Perhaps at that point Ranjith would come to his senses and declare an intern-free environment. Evangeline shrugged inwardly. You could but hope. In the meantime there was her trusty fit-and-fold. As she did every morning, she scanned the surrounding landscape for her shirtless son-in-law (prospective). There was no sign of him. In fact, there hadn't been these past few weeks, though what she had noticed recently with alarming regularity was a yellow three-wheeler with flashing lights, blue, red, blue. This morning that wasn't there either.

It was a quiet Saturday, the rain last night having washed the air clean, and the surroundings looked like a canvas freshly touched up by the artist. She could see the young cop down below at his checkpoint but that was it. So when the white vans intruded upon the landscape she noticed them immediately. They turned in at the gates of Serendipity and alarm bells began ringing in her head. Out of them debouched a stream of people, some with buckets, some with canisters.

1983. She could almost smell the petrol.

Perhaps it was a remembrance of times past. Perhaps it was the atavistic call of her Kandyan ancestors long dead, crying out for her to protect those weaker than herself. Before she knew it she found herself downstairs in the entrance hall casting about for a weapon. Seizing a multi-coloured golf umbrella from the hall-stand she wrenched open the front door.

Ten o'clock on a Saturday morning is late for the tropics, but the doors and windows to the front verandah were closed. The inhabitants of Serendipity were up, but not down. The men in the white vans were charming to Suranganee. So charming, in fact, that she forgot herself and opened the gates to them. They parked in the portico. 'Do you know what we do when there are rats in the house?' asked one of them, smiling at Suranganee. 'We smoke them out.'

'Fit and fold, shit and hold,' Evangeline prayed as she ran. Her legs almost buckled under her. 'Don't be afraid,' she whispered to herself, 'they're only your countrymen, after all.'

She arrived at the roadblock. 'Come with me!' she ordered the young cop. He looked at her, half-suppressing a smile. She looked like some bizarre extra from one of those amateur Colombo productions of *Singing in the Rain*.

'I'm your boss's wife. I command you!'

He turned his head away haughtily. No woman could speak to him like that.

She couldn't delay any further. She began running down the road. Fit and fold, shit and hold. Fit and fold, shit and hold! She burst in through the gates of Serendipity. There were droplets of rain on the bushes and the gravel in the driveway felt soft underfoot.

The men in the white van saw her glittery headband, her wobbly electro-pink bottom. They began to snigger.

'Shut up!' she screamed. 'If any of you . . .' she looked around at their assembled moon faces, 'if any of you so much as lifts a finger, you'll have to burn me first!'

They looked at each other in disbelief.

'Do you know who I am?' She struck viciously at a hibiscus bush with her umbrella, raising a small shower of droplets. 'I'm Ranjith Rodrigo's wife. Got that?'

You could almost see the doubt rippling through their minds.

'Anyone here makes a move, they'll have him to deal with. And I don't need to tell you what he's like.'

As with any mob, this one had a momentum of its own. With her umbrella she had struck accurately at its centre of gravity, the very heart of it, and managed to change its motion. When the leader turned round to get back into the van, she knew she had won. She could feel her breath moving in and out of her lungs as if through bellows.

Fit and fold, it went. Shit and hold.

Inside the house she sensed a strange thickening of the atmosphere. As if the commotion outside had somehow got in and was reverberating around the walls, trapped like flying insects. You felt there was more to come, that the play had not yet begun. She sipped the brandy Suranganee had left her with, noticing the bare floorboards, the patches on the walls where pictures had been taken off, the cardboard boxes on the floor filled with photo frames. She picked one out. It was the one of Chelvam and the Pope. She wondered at what point Ranjith would manage to take her to the Vatican.

There was a slight scuffle on the stairs and looking up she saw three very old people come down, heads bowed. Suranganee had extracted them from the small store-room next to Ganga's quarters where they had been hiding.

They were whispering to each other. Serendipity, which had seemed to them inviolable through all the ravages of the previous decade—the riots, the taxes, the land reform—had finally been breached. Now, perhaps, they could see it through the eyes of strangers. It was just another old house waiting patiently to be looted or burned or simply razed to the ground. It had ceased to have any intrinsic value: just that moment it had lost its place on the map; it was a blank space in the jigsaw, a gap in the teeth. All the more reason to move on. Adapt or die, scientists always said.

Evangeline hadn't seen her neighbours at close quarters for

at least a year and was struck immediately by how much they had aged. In fact they had aged far more in the last twenty minutes.

There was a certain awkwardness all round. What do you say to someone who has just saved your life?

'How's your bed?' asked Ganga finally.

Evangeline looked blank for a moment. Then she remembered. 'Ranjith and I were gutted to see it go. You know, Lionel specially made it for us when we got married.' Her mind clouded over for a moment with memories of happier times. 'We had a decorator in last year. He said, "Either that bed goes or I do." She looked sad.

'I remember the underside of it rather well,' said Ganga drily.

After settling the old people downstairs, Suranganee hurried off to the pavilion.

'Wake up!' she said shaking Piyumi roughly. 'Your life has just been saved. You'd better go and thank the person who saved it.'

By the time Piyumi arrived in the drawing room, her saviour was leaving.

'Any time,' Evangeline was saying. 'Any time you need help, don't be afraid to ask. I'm always up there on my balcony.' She pointed through the trees. 'Being a minister's wife must have some uses, mustn't it?'

Piyumi watched her retreating lurex bottom with fascination. 'Who's that weirdo?' she asked.

'Our neighbour,' said Ganga. 'You don't know her. Once, when you were a baby you spent a week under her bed.'

27

'Attacked?' said Debs. 'Why wasn't I informed?' Piyumi had visions of the arsonists sending out pasteboard invitation cards.

White Van Man
Requests the Pleasure of your Company
At a Riot

Dress: Optional
RSVP:PBABP
(Please bring a bottle of petrol)

'They wouldn't have dared do anything if I was there!'

Funny though this sounded, it had more than a grain of truth to it. NGOs were a widely accepted part of everyday Sri Lankan life. No one disputed the amount of good they did. For that very reason they were universally respected; also universally disliked.

Piyumi was beginning to understand how any outsider attempting to live in Sri Lanka had to try to come to terms with the strange love-hate regime under which—and only under which—they would be tolerated:

> Resist at all times that urge to do good. If you feel the insane compulsion once in a while, at least have the good sense to keep that chink in your armour, that wound in your side wide open: so people can look, and feel superior, and despise you. (Who knows, they might even stick the spear back in.) Feeling sorry they'll come to grow quite fond of you, though this is as far as it'll ever go. By helping them you have automatically put yourself on a superior plane and they will never forgive you for this. If you expect more gratification from your deeds, more bang for your bucks, please take your money elsewhere. Try Kazakhstan.

When Sinnetambe appeared at the doorway of Women in Want Piyumi assumed it was to ask about the health of his clients.

'They're okay,' Piyumi assured him. 'They were actually upstairs when the mob came.'

Sinnetambe shook his head. 'I'm glad of that. But that's not what I came about. There's a problem with the sale, Miss Segarajasingham.'

The sound of her heart pounding filled her chest. 'Has he withdrawn? Is Skanda pulling out?'

'No, nothing like that.'

She felt almost weak with relief. 'So what's the matter then?'

'You need to call him.'

'He can wait,' she said airily. 'As long as he's buying Serendipity, I really don't give a damn what else he does.'

And so before she knew it, life bounced back to normal. It was the sort of thing Colombo managed so well: attempted murder, arson and riots in the morning; gallery openings and cocktails in the evening. At times Piyumi felt she was in one of those frenzied Bollywood music videos. Every time she looked down, her costume and identity seemed to have changed: tasselled bikinis, sequinned salwars, hipster jeans, all in a day's work. And while she gyrated wildly in the same place, the scenery behind her changed too—Hindu Temples, Himalayan Peaks, Taj Mahals all zoomed up alarmingly, and just as suddenly, as they were about to engulf you they disappeared.

Most polling stations were situated in schools, so the government was declaring school holidays just before elections.

'I'm going camping with Raf and the girls,' said Percy ffinch-Percy to Marek. 'Lovely little place outside Colombo called Homogama.'

'Homagama?'

'That's right. Homogama. There are two sites, I understand. One higher, one lower. I would have preferred the high camp myself. But I think they've chosen the other. Do feel free to join.'

'I may have to go to London.'

'Oh?'

'My mother just got married.'

'What a relief for you! No one can ever call you little bastard in the playground again.'

'Are we going to Nuwara Eliya for the break?' Mrs Herath asked her sister on the phone. (The ministerial bungalow was palatial beyond words. Hi-fi, wi-fi, hot and cold running interns.)

'Don't know, dear. Depends on the elections.'

'What have elections got to do with it?'

There was a pause. 'There might be a lot of measuring up to do,' said Evangeline somewhat cagily.

The full import of this struck Mrs Herath like a blast from a hot furnace. My goodness, I might be the sister-in-law of the prime minister! My pol sambal days are over! Even as she thought this she felt a slight tinge of regret.

'We may be going to Nuwara Eliya for Easter,' said Iresha to Marek. 'Can you come? Mummy would be delighted to have you.'

'I don't know,' said Marek thoughtfully. 'I might go to London. I might stay here. Depends.'

'Depends on what?'

'I have to ask someone a question. Depends on the answer.'

'There were two calls for you today,' said Suranganee to Piyumi. 'One from your mother. One from someone who won't give his name. It's not the first time he's called.'

'I am indeed honoured,' said Piyumi, 'that I have begun once again to receive calls through your esteemed good offices.

That second caller. Tell me. Did he sound nefarious to you?'

But Suranganee had already fled.

Next day on the way home, Piyumi made Viraj stop at Galle Face Green. It was one of those rare periods when the Green was actually open for public consumption and people were strolling on the broad walk that ran above the sea wall. Old gents in baggy shorts rotated their outstretched arms vigorously as if taxiing for take-off. Young couples strolled arm in arm eating fried chickpeas out of conical paper packets fashioned from old newspapers.

An aged woman was being pushed in her wheelchair by a slatternly domestic. 'Faster!' she screamed as they picked up speed, 'Faster!' It was difficult to decide which was getting more exercise, the wheelchair or the domestic. It wasn't the old woman anyway; unless you counted her vocal chords.

Far out in the ocean you could see the irregular shapes of grey battleships smudged on a grey horizon like stamps on an airmail envelope. She couldn't decide later what it was that prompted her. Perhaps it was the feeling that her river of good fortune was about to strike rocks, that there was turbulence up ahead. She seized his arm and said: 'Marry me.'

He couldn't have heard, so she pulled him towards her and repeated, 'Marry me.'

His eyes lit up with hope. 'And we'll go abroad?'

'God, no!' she said and immediately regretted it. She

tried to smile but it was too late: he had seen the horror in her eyes.

'I mean,' she continued trying to repair the damage, 'aren't we better off here? I have the pavilion, I have my job. You have your family.'

Viraj said nothing. A small boy with a kite suddenly ran between them and they watched him disappear up the broad walk. He had never been one for words. His gym, his three-wheeler, his music: these were his modes of expression: words had never been much of a part of his vocabulary. But as with all people who were not vocal, he had an instinctive feel for the rights and wrongs of anything, the strengths and weaknesses. He knew there was an almost unbridgeable gulf between them, far wider than the open drain that ran behind his house in the watte.

It was not because she was Tamil: he was not a racist, whatever the rest of his family might be. But she was a feudal, he was not. She was older. She came from one of those families that spoke, thought and dreamt in English. Sinhala or Tamil might be their mother tongue but it was very much a second language, a language used only to speak to the servant classes.

Going abroad would have saved him. It would have wiped him clean of his antecedents, spun him crazily out of his karmic cycle. He would have learnt the flat South London vowels of the builders, the shopkeepers, the wide-boys and petty crooks. It wouldn't quite have been Knightsbridge, but as a couple they would have passed muster. In Colombo they were doomed even before they began. These thoughts were as clear to him as if they were lit up on giant billboards in the night sky. So he hugged her fiercely and said nothing.

The atmosphere had dissolved perceptibly to a greyness that was almost opaque; a greyness of cats in the dark. The battleships had long since disappeared from the horizon.

Without a word they got into the three-wheeler and drove home.

Her footsteps sounded hollow and loud on the bare floorboards. The house had gone to sleep so she switched on only the hallway light. All around, the up-ended rolls of carpet, the dismembered beds, the disembowelled almirahs cast strange jurassic shadows.

It was really not the time to be calling Skanda. Somebody should have told her that when the little glittery pieces in the kaleidoscope begin to fall the other way, they continue falling. Nothing can stop them.

He answered almost at the first ring. 'I've been trying to reach you for days.'

She could picture him by the freezer cabinet in his long cashmere coat, ready to go out.

'I'm sorry,' she said.

'We have a slight problem, Miss Segarajasingham.'

'Don't tell me you're not buying the property?'

'No, nothing like that.' He coughed delicately. 'But we will be wanting it all.'

'You're getting six-sevenths of it.'

There was silence at the other end. 'For our purposes, Miss Segarajasingham, we'll be requiring the whole property.'

And for the second time her head began to spin and she had to sit down.

'You've told me it's for a charitable purpose. Why can't I be part of that? You know I'd be happy to.'

There was a pause. 'Miss Segarajasingham, in our organization I'm just a small cog in the machinery. It's not up to me, I'm af . . .'

'No!' she shouted before she could stop herself. 'If I can't have it, you can't either!'

Ganga's word kept running through her head. Nefarious, nefarious, nefarious.

'Is that your last word on the subject?' he began to ask, but she had already put the phone down.

Lying alone on her iron bed in the pavilion that night, she might have been entombed in a pyramid, so alone did she feel. What was most bitter was that within the space of an evening she had gone from having a house, a lover, a country, to losing the lot.

Only a week back she had saved Viraj's life. Surely it was his turn to save her now? But no, he couldn't see that or wouldn't. There are hidden symmetries to these serendipitous events of our lives, she thought: it is up to us to discover them and act on them, and in so doing fulfil the pattern.

But there was another way of looking at it. What if there is only ever the one side to any story, the absolute truth cast in stone? What if all these symmetries we think we perceive are merely false patterns, spurious reflections in the mirrors of the kaleidoscope?

I have one more card to play, she thought as she drifted off into an uneasy sleep. I will not, will not let this thing beat me.

28

The great flowering trees along the road had lost their blooms in the rain. The ditches that ran on either side were filled with six inches of water and Piyumi could already see little tadpoles shooting about in them. The young cop at the roadblock raised an eyebrow at the sight of her walking, at this new method of transport. He had seen her in a car, he had seen her in a three-wheeler. He had seen her driving a three-wheeler. Next, no doubt, she'd go galloping by on a horse.

She managed to get through the guards at the gate by explaining she was a neighbour, and was shown into a small ante-room to the side of the house reserved for the general public, bare and finger-marked, a total contrast to what you might expect of a house like this. If you need any help don't hesitate to ask, the woman had said. Being a minister's wife must have some uses, mustn't it?

The minister was one of those rare politicians who had been rich long before he became important. If anyone had the money to buy Serendipity, he did. She was interrupted in her reverie by the figure at the door.

'You're Mrs Segarajasingham's daughter. Why have they shown you in here?'

'We can't thank you enough for what you did the other day,' Piyumi mumbled, following Evangeline through into the main house. She was in various shades of blue today: marine, ultramarine, navy and midnight. Her bottom wobbled fascinatingly as she walked. They entered two enormously long reception rooms, one leading into the other, with parquet floors so shiny they might have had half an inch of treacle poured on them. There were profuse arrangements of flowers all over in various shades of white, and white leather Corbusier loungers. Separating the two rooms almost like a screen was a giant polar bear, cunningly colour-coordinated. Either side of this animal hung two larger-than-life-size Keyts. To own one that size in this day and age would have been extraordinary. To own two was positively ministerial, no, mythical. (Evangeline had had them knocked up by a student at the Vibhavi Academy of Arts in his off-hours. The signatures had cost extra.)

Piyumi explained her problem.

'Ranjith, can you come in here a minute?' said Evangeline to the polar bear. 'It's our neighbour's daughter. She has a problem.'

'Oh, leave me alone, will you?' growled the polar bear. 'Can't you see I'm relaxing?'

'Ranjith!'

The minister emerged reluctantly from the other room. He did indeed look like a sort of Sri Lankan polar bear, small and curly-haired and grizzled, in the white Arya Sinhala costume that is the hallmark of every Sri Lankan politician. (Party politics dictated you were free to be in mufti in the privacy of your own home but the minister was a great believer in The Method, where you remain in character at all times.)

Just then there was a sharp intake of breath. Evangeline had discovered the beginnings of a new roll of flesh on her tummy. She sprang up. 'Must dash!' she said. 'Bit more exercising to do. I'll leave you both to it.'

The minister looked somewhat sourly at Piyumi. 'There are no more vacancies for interns,' he said. Then he noticed her legs. 'But if you care to leave your CV?'

'I haven't come about a job,' Piyumi interrupted him.

'The thing is . . . would you like to buy our house? Serendipity. The old one three doors away.'

His face took on a sharp knowing look, the look of every trader through the ages who scents a bargain, smells the desperation of the seller.

'I've seen it,' he said abruptly. 'At least my men have.' She looked surprised but he continued. 'It was in the paper a month back. They want too much for it.'

'Please,' she said. She hated to hear herself beg. 'I want someone to buy the main house so I can keep the back bit.'

He was shaking his head. 'No good,' he said firmly. He was well versed in the art of walking out the door and being dragged back in by the desperate shopkeeper. 'Besides, they tried to attack it last week. Somebody high up has their eye on it.' He got up to show the interview was at end.

Something in his supercilious tone, the cunning look in his eyes made her suddenly see red.

'And I suppose you wouldn't happen to know anything about that attack, would you?' she whispered.

'Miss Segarajasingham, why would I want to burn down my neighbour's house, when I was the one who saved you? And not for the first time either.'

'Your wife!' she wanted to shout. 'It's your wife who saved us back then. It's your wife who happened to save us again last week.' But she said nothing. It would have been almost churlish to deny him his delusions. She walked out of the house, past the obelisks, the clipped hedges, the sunken pools of this fairyland; past the tin toy guards in their painted sentry box at the gate.

'Feet!' said the young cop pointing to her legs, vastly amused with himself.

'Defeat,' she agreed, giggling hysterically.

It really was the end, even she could see that. There were no bells, no whistles, no Baroque choirs of angels to announce the fact. Only the silence of the road and the wide open arms of the giant trees, as she walked back to Serendipity, back to the dust and fall-out of a fast decaying half-life.

29

Marek could see an enormous black removals van parked in the portico of Serendipity. A strangely familiar driver in peaked cap and his somewhat elderly wall-eyed assistant were struggling with unwieldy bits of dismantled antique. On the side of the van was marked in gold lettering the words Truk-a-Luk Fine Driving. In a separate human chain, Piyumi, Suranganee and Viraj were loading the light bits. An observant bystander might have noticed the somewhat cool atmosphere prevailing in this second group.

Marek was not especially predisposed to be observant.

He had seen Piyumi and Viraj that day in the front row and that was enough: that said it all. Every time he arrived at Serendipity these days Piyumi seemed to be either absent or busy. As for Viraj, he no longer turned up at Deal Place in the mornings. No reason given, but it wasn't difficult for Marek to work out where Viraj was spending his nights.

What this meant in practical terms was a mad dash up the road every morning to cadge a lift off Percy ffinch-Percy in his tiny Maruti car. This had its own problems. There was usually Princy in the car and almost always some other exotic creature, exuding a faint aroma of frangipani and cinnamon bark and lime, who could rarely be persuaded to stick to his side of the back seat.

The old people were pottering about ineffectually trying to load the Toyota Crown.

'Good old Nizam!' said Ganga loudly whenever she came within earshot of the other group. 'I always knew he would come through at the eleventh hour.'

If Piyumi heard, she didn't react.

'I need to speak to you,' Marek whispered urgently. 'Alone.'

Piyumi looked up. Her eyes looked so sunken Marek was shocked.

'Not now!' she hissed. 'Can't you see I'm busy?'

'Then when?'

She shrugged and went back to her loading. He waited but she didn't look at him again. After a while he went away.

Mr Nizam was deep in the bowels of the house attempting to extract a cup of coffee from the cook. Ever patient, ever smiling, he was the very embodiment of that saying, 'All things come to him who waits'.

'And they want me to go and live with them up at the estate in Chilaw,' the cook was saying bitterly. 'And me a good Matara woman!'

It was tantamount to asking a Cornishwoman to relocate to Aberdeen.

'Tut, tut, tut,' said Mr Nizam soothingly. 'You know I was just thinking, maybe you could stay behind and cook for the workers? Of course I can't pay much, but . . .'

A wealth of possibilities hung on that delicious word but. The cook turned on him her famously gummy smile, sprinkled with the tiniest fluoride-blackened teeth.

'Three sugars did you say, or four?'

When the last Victor Sylvester record, the last Olivetti Portable, the last shell-case umbrella stand had been stuffed into the removals van, Viraj too began packing his few meagre belongings into his three-wheeler.

'You're not leaving?' Piyumi asked him in alarm.

He shrugged. 'I haven't seen my parents in quite a while.'

It was near midnight. Viraj drove through Gregory's Road up to the Kanatte junction. In the sickly yellow streetlight he could see the enormous ficus in the middle of the roundabout, its buttressed roots like the limbs of sacrificial victims slithering within its grasp. The white cut-outs of the minister placed right round did nothing to dispel the brooding malevolence emanating from within. Was it his imagination or did he hear a thousand sibilant whispers of little black creatures beckoning him in?

In the adjacent cemetery all was silence—even the ghosts were asleep—not even the vapour trail of a silvery head with a pointy beard, shooting off with a hiss between gravestones like a comet. What had happened to Lenin Marx Siddhu?

In crossing the roundabout Viraj had crossed once more the invisible line between Cinnamon Gardens and that other country, the one of potbellied children and standpipes and open drains. He was back once again in his watte, and it seemed to him he had been away a long time and was glad to be back.

He thought, not without a certain bitterness and not for the first time, that she had been only too willing to offer him a visa to her life in Cinnamon Gardens, but not to her life abroad; though both had been well within her power. But he was not one for regrets: it was too early in his young life for that. Years later, he would look back on her with a love she probably did nothing to deserve at the time: apart from that small matter of saving his life.

He could never put it into actual words, but he realized with pitch-perfect clarity that it was not him she wanted: it was everything he stood for, his essential Sri Lankanness: if she had been some sort of vampire able to suck these life-enriching qualities out of him she would have done so unhesitatingly, casting him aside when finished.

To be perfectly fair, he had wanted exactly the same of her. Or to be more precise he had wanted the opposite: he had wanted her foreignness. Taken together they did not constitute a recipe for the good life.

Idly, he wandered down the cul-de-sac towards Lenin Marx's tiny house. It was in darkness. But two doors down, the lights were on. As he drove past, a sharp high laugh rang out from within. It wasn't Celestina's voice. He half considered going in but it was during her working hours, it wouldn't have been polite to interrupt. And then he noticed it. In Celestina's yard, underneath a tarpaulin. Piyumi's car, its battered tail-light sticking out of a corner.

30

All day long there's been this thud! thud! thud! pounding in my head like a headache. (Actually it's more like thug! thug! thug! There's a musical undertone to it, the resonance of a whole wall vibrating like the skin of a drum.) It is the sound of club hammers connecting with eighteen-inch cabook. Whoever said these walls wouldn't last was right. They are coming down very nicely, thank you, one by one.

Nizam has put the housebreakers on price work so they'll be working through the night. It is funny how they have colonized the house already: their little scraps of coloured clothing strung from column to column in these high wide rooms like birds flying south in formation. Once there were ivory tusks and silver cabinets and gramophones on stands; now only the all-pervasive smell of dhal and onion sambal and devilled dry fish, all of which the cook dishes up out of great cauldrons for their supper.

Far away I hear the cook and Nizam singing kavi, each outdoing the other in the bawdiness of their rhyming couplets. And beneath and around, like a sort of surround-sound, the thug! thug! thug! Because the housebreakers are on through the night, and it's long past midnight and I can't sleep. And though I'm lying in this iron bed, my eyes wide open, I don't mind. Because in my mind I'm actually walking through these rooms one last time, rehearsing and re-rehearsing the lines of an accidental masterwork for posterity: I am the blind man running his fingers again and again down the face of the beloved.

(You notice I don't call this house Serendipity any more. In a week it won't be. It'll actually be the opposite: the occurrence of events by chance in an unhappy way.)

The murano chandeliers were gone, every last crystal drop. Cockroaches and beetles scuttled across yellowed patches of the wall where yellowing pictures had once been. You could see clouds of rising damp, and the stick-like branches of red rising from the ground like modern art where termites were making inroads into the cabook. The house stood like an old woman shorn of her jewellery and evening dress, blinking foolishly in the daylight.

Was it Einstein who said that all matter is merely the warping of space? That once matter has gone the space springs back, reasserting itself like a rubber ball after it has been punched?

Well, he didn't know about this house, did he? This is not just some aberration of space; it is the accretion, the repository of a hundred years of memory. Once it goes there'll only be my word for it: what I may or may not choose to say or write about it. At best those words will have the artificial shininess, the bright nursery colours of recreated legend. And they will be only words: a poor substitute for the thousand and one shades of fading actuality. Am I the only one who sees this? Or is this idea so worn, so threadbare that only I am still naïve enough to give it currency?

The first thing to come down was the roof. Eighteen-foot timbers the thickness of a man's waist brought down the main staircase on ropes. Enough wood to restock an entire forest; the fabled Forest of Nizamabad. The house is now filled with light, suffused and glowing, like the eyes of a terminal patient the day before his death.

There's this other strange fixation of mine I need to talk to you about . . . If you're my analyst you'll say that all my life I have yearned for a country figure, the way other people might yearn for a mother figure. You see, I lost my country in a fire—oh, it was a long time ago now, I was very young— and they took pity on me and farmed me out to a foster country. But these foster people aren't really much good, are they? Of course they mean well, they give you the best of everything. But I could never really digest all those parboiled values, I missed the spice of my birth mother's home cooking. So when I grew up I came back looking for her. But all I found was this little old lady, troubled but really quite happy with her own life, not particularly concerned with mine. To be perfectly fair, all she probably saw in me was this Westernized stranger with her weird accent, blundering about with no doubt the best of intentions, yet never in full possession of the unending subtleties that go to make up the life here. Maybe after twenty years of living here I might have come to some sort of understanding with her, but I wasn't given that chance, was I? Though you can't say I didn't try. Nobody told me about that Third Law of Serendipity, you see: Never think you can go about reclaiming lost countries. You will only end up losing what little country you had in the first place.

Oh, they've just turned the electricity off. It was only a formality, really, the patient was clinically dead a long while before. There was absolutely no point keeping the life-support going. Who can afford such hefty medical bills these days?

The truth is, I failed. And failed big time. It's time now to go back with my tail between my legs; though I warn you I won't go quietly. I will kick and scream. I may be down but not out. Bloody but unbowed. Any other clichés? Oh yes, I'll insist on behaving like that woman who never lets you forget her mother lives in Knightsbridge.

Tomorrow I'll go reclaim my car. It was promised for the duration of my stay. Then I'll hand in my report. Then I'll give them notice. Then I'll get the hell out.

31

There was a throb of expectancy in the watte, the faintest shiver of anticipation in the smoky morning air. Celestina was in her yard, all blowsy and familiar in a long gown of some shiny material. She beamed when she saw who it was.

The tarpaulin lay neatly folded on the ground.

'Where's the car?' asked Viraj.

'Where's the girlfriend?' countered Celestina archly. 'I told her to bring it back by eleven the latest.' She looked importantly at a large orange plastic watch strapped onto her wrist. 'She's going to be late, and they need it to get to the stadium.'

'Who's they?'

Celestina looked at him as if he was a little simple or something. 'Lenin's men, of course.'

And suddenly the kaleidoscope took a quarter turn and another picture sprang out of nowhere, little scraps of blue and gold and red, like a bunch of flowers flourished under your nose by a magician. And he realized how cheap the price of treason was that year on the open market: they had all bought it: it had seemed such excellent value at the time.

She looked at him coquettishly. 'Do you want to come in for a little something? A little hot cup of Milo, maybe?'

He spat on the ground in front of her.

'I wouldn't come in if you paid me,' he said and began to run.

Marek had been ringing the bell for five minutes before he realized there was no one to open the gate. He could hear the workers hammering inside but opening gates was obviously not in their job description. Piyumi must be in there too, getting ready for work. Then he saw the battered green car coming up the road with her inside.

He flagged it down.

'I have to get to work,' she said crossly. 'I'm late enough as it is.'

'Please. I have to talk to you.'

She turned the engine off. 'Five minutes,' she said. He opened the passenger door and got in.

'You're sitting on my report.' She pulled out a bulky folder from under him.

'I see you got the car back, then?'

'Marek,' she said, 'I don't have all day to sit here discussing the car. What is it you wanted to say?'

Up ahead they could hear a commotion at the minister's house. A florist's van had arrived.

'I've never seen so many garlands,' Marek murmured. 'For

the end of the speech, when ardent fans rush onstage to garland him. All that spontaneity takes a lot of planning.'

'I've been thinking,' said Marek. 'You lost the house. Still, you got your share from the sale.' He looked around hopelessly. 'I have money too . . .'

The florist's van reversed out and there was a clatter as the yellow barriers were wheeled into place to close the road.

'Now look what you've done,' she said annoyed. 'We're stuck here another ten minutes.' Somewhere in the car, a mobile began to ring. That's odd, she thought absently, I don't own a mobile. Marek doesn't either.

'What I wanted to say is, will you marry me?'

She looked at him and the lines around her mouth softened. She had never been more in love with him than at that moment. Up the road they could see the minister's convoy beginning to leave his gates, the young cop saluting.

The mobile appeared to be ringing in the boot. And then it came to her. The possibility that her entire life had been just a preamble, after all, to this chance flowing together of events, the grim possibilities that lay like sharp rocks below the water. She turned to Marek.

'Get out,' she said.

'But . . .' He looked so hurt, so vulnerable.

'Get out!' she yelled again angrily. Opening his door, she pushed him out. He looked at her uncomprehendingly, like a dumb animal prodded with a stick. She slammed the door shut.

'Please,' he whispered through the window. 'I love you.' He was almost in tears.

But her mind had already swum out from beneath the crushing weight of all mortal obligation. It was the fish in the tsunami, floating free, skimming waves, flying from crest to crest in a streak of diagonal silver.

Up ahead she imagined she saw the young cop looking in her direction flirtatiously. She checked in the mirror to see her lipstick was all right. Sweeping her hair back in one magnificent movement, she pressed down hard on the gas.

Marek stood on the verge open-mouthed, watching the car hurtle towards the roadblock. Behind him he heard a three-wheeler screeching to a stop. A figure leapt out and a pair of strong arms grappled with him. He felt himself falling into the tadpole-filled ditch.

'Boom!'

'What was that dear?' 'Nothing, dear. Just a bomb.'

'A bomb? Fuck!'

'Don't swear, dear.'

'Bomb-fuck-a-boom-fuck-a-bomb!'

'Now you're just being crude, dear.'

32

The loss of Ranjith Rodrigo, the party's most charismatic member, changed the course of history, the voters sweeping the opposition into power on a wave of passive aggressiveness or tide of apathy, depending on which way you looked at it. (If they couldn't elect the man they wanted, they might as well elect anybody.)

The new government met one last time before its inauguration, at the Fuk-a-Luk Café.

Their leader put on his spectacles. 'Ranjith Rodrigo was a great man,' he said. 'It was he the gods had their eye on to lead this country. I am here in his place only because of an accident of chance, or serendipity. Call it what you will.'

'Accident?' muttered the shadow minister of defence from somewhere near the back. 'Did he say accident?' He gave a snort. Or it might have been the extra-strength garlic in the kang-kung.

'So I would ask you to raise your cups and toast him.' ('But he is toast,' murmured the shadow minister for food.)

Up and down the tables there was a great clicking and

clacking of porcelain thimbles, and muted murmurs over the pale green tea of Ranjith Rodrigo, Ranjith Rodrigo . . .

'This will be the last time we meet here,' continued the leader gloomily. 'I'm afraid we're forced to move on to higher things. From now on it's the Hilton for us.' He folded his spectacles neatly by the side of his bowl and chopsticks. 'So I have ordered double helpings of chilli paste all round. To ease your passage.'

'My report!' said Debs disconsolately. 'Where's my report?'

The girls at Women in Want rallied round, comforting her in her great bereavement.

'May she rest in peace,' said Percy ffinch-Percy.

'May she rest in pieces,' breathed Fernando, fervently crossing himself.

33

A three-wheeler was perhaps not the best method of getting to the airport. Marek had arrived in the country with very little in the first place: so now there was only a small suitcase wedged in the back with him, and a backpack. The school had been most understanding in the circumstances.

All along the Panchikawatte Road, sandwiched inbetween motor spares shops and timber yards, the cut-outs loomed larger than ever. Elections were over. Next on the agenda was the State Funeral, a far more pleasurable event as far as the populace was concerned. The dead minister lived on (so to speak) in his embalmed state, rushing hither and thither in unseemly haste from Galle to Jaffna, Puttalam to Trinco, for frenzied crowds to pay their last respects. Everybody loves a good funeral. It was the closest thing the country would get to the death of a Diana or a Michael Jackson.

The rattle and roll of the three-wheeler precluded conversation, but in any case the two men were not disposed to do much talking. They shared a carton of Body-Plus, taking alternate swigs, passing it back and forth. The bond between them had deepened these last few days.

If only I had said yes, thought Viraj sadly.

If only she had said yes, thought Marek sadly. So many lives might have been saved.

Viraj had already forgotten that the chain of command leading to these deaths passed directly through him, in a seemingly inexorable line of dots from Piyumi all the way back to those shadowy killers in the mean streets of London. This fact was no longer important: it had had its five minutes. It was already wiped clean off the hard disk, erased from the memory of the main frame.

I tried to save her, Viraj would later say. I ran. I didn't get there in time, that's all. It was a good thing for him his God was not that terrible and terrifying God of the ancient Jewish scriptures, unyielding and implacable, who never forgave, who never forgot. He was, indeed, the child of a lesser God— a smiling Third World one—who had his hands full merely trying to decide whether your child was to be born to feudal pomp or foetid squalor (and who was to pay for his school uniform anyway?) and whether your grandmother was to die on the floor of the General Hospital for want of a bed, or whether she was to end her days in privately air-conditioned splendour at the Apollo.

As for Marek, the all-too brief span of his acquaintance with Piyumi had been characterized by an unending series of fortuitous coincidences. In that short time he had lived many lives to the full, vicariously through her: it was just a pity none of them had been his own. It had always seemed obvious to him that there must be some divinely preordained symmetry, a strange beauty to the pattern of their conjoined lives. She had chosen to think otherwise. In fact she had gone further, snatching up the kaleidoscope, shaking it vigorously and smashing it to the ground. Or could it just be that she had seen another pattern there, recondite and obscure, so esoteric no one else could see it? And was her death then merely the last piece, the last shimmering gold fleck placed precisely and carefully, to be repeated many times in the mirror?

Because they were men, these grave thoughts were interspersed, like occasional bursts of static on TV, with other serious thoughts like What's for lunch? and I can't believe it, that idiot just tried to cut us!

Somewhere near the stadium Viraj finished the last of the Body-Plus and chucked the carton out on the road where it hit the nose of a passing pariah dog. Marek was thinking of what lay ahead. The new leaves would be out on Clapham Common; and with them the sunbathers, their winter skin fresh and green, as yet unexposed to the sun. He saw Dennis and his mother hand in hand, blown aimlessly about the bare spaces of the Common by gusts of wind. She was in the thick black winter coat she always wore come rain or shine, her Sunday morning church coat.

He thought of the Bed and Breakfast that lay in wait.

As the road wound on, the repeated face on the cut-outs seemed to change. Was it his imagination or was the minister smiling at him? Suddenly, to his astonishment, he saw one particular cut-out where the minister was pointing his finger directly at him, like in that old poster of Kitchener. Your country needs you. And what country might that be?

He leant forward and tapped Viraj on the shoulder. 'Turn this thing round,' he said. 'You know what? I think maybe I'll stick around for a little, after all.'

ACKNOWLEDGEMENTS

My grateful thanks to Seela Wijewardene for her invaluable comments on this manuscript, and to Adam Smyth who fought valiantly for extra commas and hyphens. Needless to say, he lost. ('They're my mistakes,' I said. 'Let me keep them.') To the Wife and Kids for putting up with a miserable old cuss during the writing of this book; and of course to Kumar at magical Closenberg Hotel, Galle, where much of it was written.